MW01229469

STREET LAMPS

K R Albers

Man of Few Words Publishing

Part One

The scene was set so perfectly. The smoke rose from the ends of his fingertips, only breaking long enough for him to take another drag. He sat back in his chair, pulled his arms up and his hands to the back of his head. He stared to the typewriter as if he were worshipping at an altar; perfect lines of ink-blotted words from top to bottom. He smiled, more of exhausted content than joy. He pulled his thick frames from his nose and set them atop a stack of loose papers on the corner of his desk. Whether he was finished or not, it was time for a break; his fingers bent into submission from hours and hours of typing. And as his mind still raced of plot twists and torrid love affairs, he made his way down the long hallway that led to his apartment's kitchen. Just as he reached the sink to empty his coffee cup for a chance at the new pot brewing, he took a scan of the room. A skillet with half-fried eggs sat atop the stove, and toast popped up from the toaster awaited being plucked up and eaten. He laughed to himself for having completely abandoned a midnight snack, or lunch as some would call it, because a character name had come to him.

In the living room set just off the kitchen, the blue light of a TV flashed in and out against the kitchen wall. He stepped into the room, grabbing the remote for a quick scan of the channels; infomercials and sex hot lines were all he found. He raised his mug to his lips and took a sip, standing there, hand on hip, as if waiting for something to happen. These were the only moments reality would creep into his mind; the only time she ever came calling.

Breaking him from his daydream was the ringing of the telephone. He stared angrily at the receiver perched up on the kitchen wall. Seven rings before it quit. His frame budged not an inch toward it, his tired eyes just examining for the slightest vibration that came with each ring. His focus turned back to the infomercial on the television: kitchen knives that could cut you out of handcuffs. A smile crept onto his face watching the expressions of the actors in the commercial, for the volume was down and he was going solely on lip reading.

"Amazing," he whispered as he went for another sip. "Maybe I should work this in somewhere, just for a laugh."

Again came the ringing from the kitchen. He stood puzzled. A laundry list of creditors and congressman looking for his vote shot through his head, desperately trying to figure out who would be calling at this hour. 'What time is it in India?' he thought to himself.

Seven rings and it stopped. Still, his frame never changed, hand on hip and milking a cup of coffee. He grew slightly more aggravated now, as his ten-minute break was becoming riddled with questions of who the incessant late night caller could be.

Determined to not stray from his recent victories on the typewriter, he trod back down the hall towards his prison cell to lock himself away for a few more hours. Just as he reached the threshold, the echo down the hall was that of the telephone hanging in the kitchen.

"Damnit," he whispered. This was the third call. With each phone call, he could sense those in the neighboring apartments were waking and growing more and more agitated. They were sitting up in bed, cursing him. They were slapping every inch of their night table's surface to find their watch and check what time exactly it was that their sleep was being interrupted. They were sliding into bathrobes and slipping into their slippers, making their way for the door to come and complain.

He rushed back down the hall, his lanky legs almost tangling underneath him in his hurried state. He reached out for the telephone at ring number four. He picked it up.

Before answering, he held for a beat. He could feel the anger in his neighbors subsiding; them slipping back into bed, still cursing his name, but happy the ringing had stopped.

"Hello?" he questioned as he lifted the receiver to his ear.

"Michael! Finally," a young and energetic voice on the other end began. "What took so long man? I mean, I know you weren't sleeping."

A sigh came over him, though he wasn't sure just what exact feeling was behind it: relief, aggravation, or guilt. It was his little brother, Sam, on the line.

After a beat, Michael answered, "Sam. What are you doing calling so late, man? Besides trying to get me kicked out of my apartment for disturbing the peace."

"Oh, sorry, Michael," his voice fell to an almost ashamed tone. "I was just calling to tell you my flight landed safely back home. Remember, you told me to call you when I landed?"

His mind searched through the past few days to find the conversation in question. There was a gross jumble of coffee, cigarettes, dialogue, a phone call with his editor, and, yes, the telephone conversation with Sam.

"Oh, yeah. Well, good news. How was the flight?"

Sam took a second before answering, perturbed by the length of time it took his brother to remember a conversation they had just had hours ago.

"It was awful. Lady next to me was coughing on me the whole time, and someone had a baby on the plane. Not sure what exactly they were feeding that kid, but we were all guessing after about an hour." Sam laughed at the joke he made trying to lighten the tone of the conversation.

"That's good, Sam. Listen man, I was right in the middle of something here and I really should get back," Michael rattled off, not even taking a second to comprehend what Sam was trying to do by making the joke.

"Damn, Mike," was all Sam said. There was an awkward pause while Michael searched for the right thing to say. Clearly, he had aggravated his little brother.

"I mean, I was just in the city for the third time this year, and you can't even have dinner with me? Can't even crawl down to the bar on your block to have a drink? I don't know what your deal is, man, but I'm done trying."

"Sammy, come on…" Michael began to apologize but he was cut short by the anger that was brewing on the other end of the line.

"No, Mike! Listen, alright, we all get it. You have things you're working out, or you're really deep into your book, or your screenplay, or whatever you're working on now. You don't have time, and you're not willing to make time to see your family. I get it!"

Michael took a minute. Sam was dead on.

"Anyway, I keep hoping that one of these times I come, you'll come out and we can talk. I know the Amy thing…"

"Hey!" Michael cut him off short. "Don't start with me, man!"

"Listen, Mike, I get it." Sam waited a beat, knowing that he had struck a nerve mentioning Michael's ex-fiancée. "Mike, mom's gonna ask me if I saw you. She's gonna ask, and I'm not going to lie to her anymore. Sooner or later, you are going to have to realize that we aren't going to cover for you anymore." The 'we' Sam was referring to was the other four brothers and sisters the two shared. "Lily comes to town, you won't see her. I come to town, I don't see you. We are all going to quit trying at some point. And then what? And then what, Mike?"

"Sam, listen…" Again, Michael was cut off.

"No, Michael, you listen. We have to read your books to even begin to assume that we know you anymore. It's seems like years since you've been home. We all miss you, but…" a long pause, "…I'm done trying."

Sam hung up the phone, and Michael stood a moment. The faces of his two brothers and three sisters flashed before his eyes; then, the face of his mother.

He hung up the receiver and walked back down the hall to

the room where his typewriter sat. 'Back to work,' he thought.

The heavy blanket that he draped over the window in the room where he wrote normally kept all the light of the day out. This way, he couldn't tell if it was night or day, as the actual time didn't apply to him when he was writing; every second of every day he was on the clock. But, as he tilted back his desk chair, he could see on the right seam a bit of the morning sunrise creeping back through. He stood and went to the window, frustrated with the paper in front of him. He had made no progress since the telephone conversation with his brother. As he made it to the window, it was that glorious time of night/early morning where the darkness was still heavier than the light, and the streetlamps still threw their rings down onto the pavement, but now amongst purple light instead of a black night. He scanned the street. A block or two down, the neon lights outside the bars were beginning to fade out. A few scattered patrons were making their way up and down the streets, trying to get home. He looked back to his typewriter, then made his way back over to it. The last line on the page read: "There she sat, so splendidly plain." His eyes went back to the window, as she began walking through his mind. Those big blue eyes, piercing and pure; that dirty blonde hair falling all about her face as she lay down to sleep. His ears perked up as something from the street began to catch his attention. After a few seconds, he knew exactly what that sound was: heels clicking on the pavement.

He rushed to the window and drew back the blanket just enough so that he could see down onto the street while still being hidden himself. He searched up and down looking for the woman to whom the heels belonged. The sound had stopped and he was struggling to find her.

Then, there, just below the streetlamp right outside his window she stood. His eyes locked on her, studying everything about her to find a discerning feature. She wore a black dress, it was a short cocktail dress. Her hair's color was a bit construed by the colors thrown from the sunrise, but it appeared to be blonde.

His eyes then went to her feet, and those heels that had called out to him. They were a bright yellow color, almost glowing they were so bright. He instantly recognized them; Amy had heels like that. He pressed his face to the glass as all the pieces were coming together, leading him to believe it was Amy standing just outside his apartment. The woman slowly began looking up, examining the windows of the all the apartments on his building. The sun's brightness was strengthening, and he could make out features of her face. Her soft chin and cheekbones caught the streetlamp and illuminated her eyes, her bright blue eyes.

He stood back from the window, the blanket falling back against it. 'That can't be her' he thought. 'How would she know where I live? It's been years since I've even spoken with her.'

He slowly pulled the blanket back away from the window and looked down onto the street, being very careful to not get too close to the window. And there she stood, looking directly at his window. He froze, it was her! She was looking right at him!

The woman on the street made her way to the door of his building, and he watched as she walked in. Panic began to set in. 'What is she doing here?', 'What do I say?', 'What is she going to say?', and then finally 'Oh my God, she's coming home to me.'

He ran to his desk and lit up a cigarette. His pulse was racing, and he eagerly awaited a knock at his door. Puffing heavily, he began to slowly walk down the hall toward the front door. As he approached the door, his steps began slowing until finally he was at a stand still five steps from the door. He waited.

After a few minutes, he could hear the clicking outside the door, just down the hall. Slowly, the clicking became louder and more frequent. His fists clenched as he knew she was approaching. Finally, the clicking was like a roar in his ears, and he knew she was close. Then, the clicking stopped. He could hear her just outside his door, her faint breaths amplified in his ears. Another puff of his cigarette, the anticipation was driving him insane. He went to the door, and pressed his hands to the knob. He was waiting for her to knock, for her to say something, for her to do anything.

Minutes felt like hours. He slowly pressed his head to the peephole. His tired eyes took a second to focus, and then it was clear. There was no one outside his door. He flung it open in a panic. He stepped out into the hall, and looked up and down. Nothing.

Part Two

There was an intense banging at the front door. He woke in a stir, flinging the blankets from his bed. The banging was also constant, and increasingly loud.

"Mikey," a voice yelled from the other side of the door. "Hey, Mikey! Wake up man, I got a schedule to keep!"

Michael made his way to the door. He recognized the voice, and was eager to get the door open and the voice silenced.

"You would think discretion is important in your field of work," Michael said as he flung the door open.

"Hey, I gotta do what I gotta do to keep my schedule," a small, greasy man exclaimed as he barged into the apartment. "Besides, do you think it's a secret or something, Hemingway?"

His name was Vince. He was a little fellow with a mouth much bigger than he needed. His tongue was sharp and his temper was short. His dark black hair was slicked back, and a cigarette was tucked behind his ear.

"You got cash today or what? A man's good faith tends to run out, you know, this isn't charity."

"Yeah, I have cash. Let me go get it," Michael said as he turned away to retrieve his wallet from the bedroom.

"How's the book coming there Mikey? Another worst seller," Vince chuckled. He was the kind of guy who loved to laugh at his own jokes. Most of the time, he was the only one laughing.

Walking back into the living room where Vince had made himself at home, Michael answered: "It's coming along. Should pay the bills."

"Well, that's good. That's good. Job security for me, eh?" Again, he chuckled at his wittiness. "Listen, you know, at any point here we can bump you up to some harder stuff and get that book written a lot faster."

He pulled a small plastic bag from inside his leather jacket as he made the recommendation. A white powder sat inside the bag. He dangled it out in front of Michael's face for a minute before Michael answered.

"Nah, just the usual alright."

Vince swapped the white powder for another bag filled with pot. He set it down on the coffee table that sat in front of the couch and stood up.

"Listen, I'm just saying, Mikey, when you are ready to step up, I have the good stuff. I mean, how do you think anything gets done in this town? I got lawyers, doctors, musicians, writers, directors, all on my payroll."

"Good to know, Vince. Good to know. Now, I'm sure you have other appointments to keep?"

Vince began to head for the door. He took one quick scan of the room, now that the business part of the visit was over.

"When's the last time you left the apartment, Mikey? Jeez."

"It's been a few days, but it's fine. None of your concern Vince."

"I'm just saying…" Vince to a look at Michael before continuing, "…You stink, buddy."

"Goodbye, Vince."

Michael shoved Vince out the door and shut it behind him.

The course of a day for him usually went as such: wake leisurely in the mid-afternoon, make the first pot of coffee, eat if he felt so inclined, and write. With the coffee pot full and a cigarette hanging from his lips, he took a moment to ponder what Vince had said. He looked around himself, nothing too incredibly filthy or atrocious, but obviously unkempt. His fingers were blotched with ink and white out spots, yellow-brown circles on his index and middle finger from where the cigarettes sat. He was compelled to venture out and get some fresh air, but as he looked down the hall, the minute he saw his typewriter sitting there, he was enthralled with lines and brainstorms.

Filling his mug and finishing his cigarette, he began back down the hall to the room where he would peck his day away. He walked into the room and sat at the desk. Putting his glasses on, he examined the last few lines he had written. He read them several times back to himself, then several times aloud. This process helped him jump right back in to where he had left off.

The next few hours were a blur of page after page, correction after correction, and the occasional trip back down the hall to fill his mug or start another pot. His last venture down the hall led him to catch a glimpse of the time as it read on the microwave perched above his stove. 'Damn' he thought to himself'. Four thirty.

At a quarter to five every evening, his downstairs neighbor would arrive home from her waitress job, two screaming kids in tow, and they would have dinner and spend the bulk of the evening playing and being loud. This was the block of time everyday when Vince's delivery would come into play. He couldn't concentrate enough to sit at his typewriter with all the noise coming from downstairs.

He went back into his office, and turned out the desk lamp positioned over his typewriter. He closed his door on the way out, and walked back down the hall to the living room. Just under the television sat an old record player. He thumbed through the cabinets on either side of the hi-fi to choose an album to listen to; today he decided on a Wilco album; Yankee Hotel Foxtrot. He carefully pulled the record from its sheath and placed it on the hi-fi. He moved to the couch after turning the volume up. Extinguishing the lamps on either side of the couch, he sunk into his self-dented cushions and melted down into a lump. He took the bag Vince had sold him and very cautiously rolled himself some joints.

Just as the first track of the album kicked in, he was drifting away into his mind, where he would sit through the entirety of the album and contemplate in expansive detail every place his story may lead. The current novel he was working on revolved around the story of a woman struggling to find herself. She was modeled very closely after Amy; in fact, most of his female characters were. She was a thirty-something struggling to deal with the idea of being alone for the holidays for the first time since her high school years. She was always the prototypical "girlfriend", always in relationships, and always working to be happy in that relationship.

As the record came to a halt, he snapped out of his plot-induced coma. He stumbled to the hi-fi just long enough to switch over to another album; Neutral Milk Hotel. As he made his way back to the couch, the record kicked in again. He often went immediately back into his storyline after an album change, but sometimes he would stutter in finding his place back. Sometimes he would revert to stories already written, sometimes he would revert to ideas he had spent time discussing with his editor; but, most of the time he went back to Amy.

It was raining the last time he saw her in the flesh. She was getting on the train, heading back to her hometown where her parents were waiting for her. He was a writer by trade, and so he felt he could always say the right things at the right times. Through the expanse of a three-year relationship, he had done just that. Every tense moment calmed by a great line.

But, that night, he was speechless, absolutely speechless. They both knew why she was leaving, and they both knew it was for the right reasons. He was supposed to be an adult. He was pushing thirty and had no steady job. She was pushing thirty and was absolutely miserable with the choices she had made in her life, from her major in college to her current job. So it seemed pretty cut and dry; simple decisions that needed to be made. But, he couldn't understand why he was taking it so hard.

The train was leaving, and he could see the seat where she sat as she began pulling farther and farther away from him. In great novels, scenes like this always end up with him chasing down the train, or with her face pressed against the glass and a single tear would stream down her cheek. But, there was none of that. She didn't even look back at him as she pulled out of sight, and he did not run.

As the second album came to an end, and the needle jumped to find its place, he snapped out of his head and back into reality. He wiped the tears that were streaming down his face, a common occurrence after these trips down memory lane.

He stood slowly and walked over to the hi-fi. He pulled the needle off the record and turned the machine off. He listened for a beat as he glanced back to the microwave. Seven thirty was the time she began calming the children down for bedtime. He heard nothing from underneath him. As he put the albums back into the cabinet, his mind began to snap back into writing mode. He went to the kitchen to start another pot of coffee, and then back down the hall to begin the night's work.

It was well past midnight, and he had been working nonstop since around eight o'clock. He stood to stretch his legs, reaching his arms high towards the ceiling. His mind was exhausted, but as he looked at the fresh stack of papers sitting next to the typewriter, he found himself very satisfied. Another twenty or so pages and he would have enough written to show his editor, a feat he dreaded more and more with each meeting.

He had some success with his first novel. It was an uplifting story of a young man struggling with his parent's abusive relationship. The story struck a chord with a decent sized group, and he found himself not only a published author, but also receiving acclaim for his work.

However, since then, his luck has been on the decline. The bulk of the first book was written over the course of a few years in his mid-twenties. This was a time when he was dating Amy, and she was supporting the two of them financially. They had broken up shortly after the book's completion, and well before the book was ever picked up for publishing. Though his first book's success had warranted him the finances to not have to work and focus primarily on writing, none of his recent projects have gotten any positive feedback from his publisher.

His editor, Frank, was his only buffer between himself and the decision makers at the publishing house. Over the past few years, Frank has shot down a dozen or more projects.

Slightly refreshed from stretching his legs, Michael lit a cigarette and strolled back down the hall, empty coffee mug in hand. He laughed to himself, contemplating the fact that he wouldn't be receiving his security deposit back when he moved out of this apartment. For years, he has been trudging this same path, from kitchen to office and back, so much so that the carpet was surely wearing thin and distinct pathways were being forged.

He had been writing steadily on this new project for three weeks. He was nearly a hundred pages in, and the plot was distinctly in place. He was dreading the phone call that he would have to make in the morning to Frank. He had spent night and day pouring himself into this new book, and in five minutes, Frank can completely throw it out the window.

He put down the coffee mug and made his way back down the hall, this time stopping off in the bathroom for a second. He turned the water on and cupped his hands underneath; the shock of cold water on his face was a perfect jump starter for another few hours of writing.

As he stood back upright, he slowly focused in on his face. His tired eyes were sunken in with darkness circling them. His beard was coming in quite nicely, not that he had been focusing on any type of grooming over the past few weeks. It was scraggly and heavier in spots. His brown hair was growing quickly as well, as it now fell just at his shoulders.

'Don't really recognize this guy,' he thought. His mind flashed back a few years, rifling through images of him; his short clean cut period, his shaggy beard and long hair hippie days. He refocused on his face again. The self-inflicted stress he was under was really starting to take its toll. Small lines were beginning to bunch around his eyes and the corners of his mouth. The gray hairs were starting to pierce through the bush of brown on the top of his head.

'Not really book sleeve picture material," he laughed.

When he looked really closely, he could see flashes of his father in his own face. When he noticed those features, even if only for a moment, he would focus on them for minutes at a time, wanting them to stay and become more prominent. He missed his father.

A car accident had taken his father from them five years ago. It was a very difficult time for the entire family back then. It was not long after that accident that Michael began distancing himself from the family, the pain of seeing his father's face in his brothers was overwhelming at times.

'Don't waste your time,' he told himself as he thrust his cupped hands back into his face, the cold water sending a chill down his spine. 'You've got work to do.'

He dried his face with the towel hanging next to the sink and stepped back into the hallway. He headed down to the kitchen to retrieve his mug of coffee and then back to the office. Back to work, yet again.

Part Three

Some assume that writers do not dream. They spend their days thumbing through their imagination looking for a story to tell and characters to develop.

Some assume that writers dream intensely every night; their imaginations so in tune with reality that they cannot help but constantly be inspired.

Michael was the former. When he was writing, his level of exhaustion was always so elevated that even if he would dream, he would not remember. Once his head hit the pillow, he would be completely gone. That is, until recently.

Since the onset of this new book, due solely to the premise he assumed, he had been dreaming a lot about Amy. This was always in the back of his head as he slaved over his typewriter, and often jotted notes in the early hours of the morning after waking from one of these dreams.

He stood from his desk and walked over to the window. He peeked out to gauge the time, assuming the early morning hours based on how dark it still was. The neon lights from the bars were still fully blazing as well, and the streets were busy.   He thought back to last night, when he had caught a glimpse of that woman down on the street, the woman he assumed was Amy. He gazed at the ring from the streetlamp where she stood, wanting so badly to see her there.

He lit a cigarette, grabbed his coffee mug and headed back out into the kitchen. He peeked into the fridge to see if there was anything in there to satisfy the slight rumble in his stomach. He scratched away at his beard, frustrated in having nothing in his fridge that wasn't expired or well past its prime. He contemplated going down the street to the little diner on the corner to have a bite to eat. Another drag from his cigarette and a sip from his coffee and he had convinced himself it was a bad idea.

He flipped through the channels on the television in the living room, once again finding nothing of value or importance. He did focus for a beat on the scantily clad women in the sex hot line ad. A man's mind tends to wander when it has been a while since he has been with a woman. But, just as quickly as it was dangled in front of him, the commercial was over and it was on to an infomercial for a food processor with blades so sharp it could dice a piece of firewood.

He tossed the remote back down onto the couch and turned back to the hallway. He walked the sixteen steps (yes, he had counted several times) back to his office to lock himself away for a few more hours before he was completely exhausted and to his breaking point.

Just as he pushed open the office door, he heard a noise; it was a very familiar noise; a warm sounding pop, like the amplifying tubes of the hi-fi warming up. He stopped dead in his tracks. In his mind, there were a million noises and odd creaks he had heard this apartment make in the middle of the night. He rifled through them quickly to justify the noise. He wasn't positive, but he was sure enough that any number of them could be the culprit.

He moved on to the desk chair and sat down. He reached for his glasses when he heard the scratch of the needle finding its mark on the record. There was no doubt in his mind that it was his hi-fi in the living room. Someone was in there.

He stood abruptly. Slowly, the sweeping strings of a classical arrangement came bleeding down the halls and into his office. He took a step toward the hallway when the horns came in. He couldn't put his finger on the composition, though he had definitely heard it before.

Once out in the hallway, a very sweet smell was growing stronger and stronger. He knew it immediately; it was a very potent French perfume he had bought for Amy the last Christmas they spent together. His eyes welled up as his feet drew him closer to the living room.

The music softened as he turned the corner to see her. And there she stood, in the middle of his living room. She wore the black cocktail dress he had seen her in the night before. Her bright yellow heels were uniformly sitting empty at the front door; she used to take her shoes off when she would come in. She was crying. Her makeup ran from her eyes, black streaks meeting just under her chin. Her hair was tossled as if she had just come in from a windy night, and those blue eyes shined from the flickering light of a roaring fire in the fireplace.

He stopped dead in his tracks. This scene was all too familiar to him. He recognized this exact scene from recent dreams he had had, and he was sure he would be waking shortly.

"Michael," she whispered in a soft, broken voice.

"This isn't real, Amy," his voice cracked as well as he spoke. "I'm going to wake up and you will be gone again."

"No, Michael. Not this time," she assured him.

She began walking toward him, now only steps away.

The dream had never gotten this far before, and in his mind Michael was wondering when it would end.

"Michael, I made so many mistakes. We made so many mistakes," she began crying. Just as she stood before him, she took his hands and spoke again.

"I'm here now, to make up for those mistakes."

He broke out in tears as she spoke, her soft hands so warm in his. She always had such soft hands. Surely, this was really happening.

"I saw you last night peeking out the window at me," she said.

"Was that really you?" he could hardly control himself. "I thought it was you, but I thought I was crazy. I heard your heels coming down the hall, but then you were gone."

"I didn't know if you would want to see me, Michael. I

didn't know if you would want me."

He touched her face ever so slightly to see if she was real. His other hand joined and he brushed the tears off her cheek.

He pulled her in for a kiss. He pressed his chapped, broken lips against hers. So soft and sweet, she held her mouth against his for a second.

He pulled away, the tears flowing like a river down his cheeks. He had waited so long for this...

He composed himself long enough to speak.

"I want you, Amy. My God do I want you."

Quickly the music turned from a soft symphony to the blaring of an alarm clock. The screeching rang out in his ears and the entire scene faded to a bright white. He opened his eyes to find he was alone in bed.

The alarm kept ringing out as he took a moment to grasp the situation, and realize he had been dreaming after all.

A normal person would describe it as nerves. That is, the feeling in the pit of his stomach as he picked up the telephone to call Frank and set up an appointment to show him the new writings.

Rang once, rang twice. 'Come on, Frank.'

"Frank Monroe," he answered.

"Hey, Frank. It's Michael Walker."

"Michael. Hey, how have you been? It's been a few weeks since I've heard from you. What have you got for me?"

Frank knew when he got a phone call from Michael that it was to see new writing. Michael was not a social guy, and also not a very astute businessman. The only contact they ever had was when a deal was being worked out, or Michael had a fresh idea.

"Well, I have some pages I'd like you to see. Can we get together sometime soon?" He worried his nerves were getting the best of him. His voice fluttered a bit, much like a pre-pubescent boy with a crush on his teacher answering a question in class.

"Listen, Michael. I got a pretty full plate right now. Don't take this the wrong way, but why don't you just fax the pages to my office."

That was a death sentence. Michael knew it.

"Hey, Frank. Come on man. I know I haven't been knocking you over lately, but this new project is gonna be the one. Just give me a half hour. I'll come downtown and we'll get a drink."

There was a long pause as Michael waited for an answer.

"Alright, Michael. Let's say an hour? Meet me at the usual?"

"Thanks, Frank. I'll see you soon."

Michael hung up the phone and raced down the hall to get the papers together. He gathered up pages from a few of the chapters he had finished, as well as a few from the fresher chapters that weren't complete. He shoved them into a file folder and then into a briefcase. He raced back down the hall to shower, for the first time in days, and get ready.

It was in no way a booming metropolis, not by any means in fact. But the city of Bloomington had its perks. The buildings never stretched taller than fifteen stories, and the local colleges kept the atmosphere current and vibrant. Michael hailed a taxi and began making his way downtown to meet with his editor. He wore his best suit, which by a businessman's standards was an old suit or a "Saturday" suit. Gray blazer and slacks with a red tie, his thick black glasses sat on his nose; his beard, though combed through, still raggedy and his hair clean.

His leg always shook the entire way to these meetings; so much so that the cab driver would often peer back over his shoulder to make sure he wasn't having a seizure. He meticulously straightened his tie and pulled up his socks. The meeting could not come fast enough.

He stepped out of the cab after paying the driver and he headed into the bar, scanning the dim room for Frank. He spotted him sitting alone in a corner booth, waving to Michael.

As usual, Frank had a gin and tonic sitting both in front of himself and one across the table for Michael.

A firm handshake and then, "Great to see you, Michael. How have you been? Busy?"

"Hey, Frank," Michael began sitting. "Yeah, I've got a new one to show you."

The two rarely wasted much time on chitchat, as Frank was a man with a full day planner and Michael rarely spent more than two hours consecutively outside of his apartment. Michael cracked the briefcase and handed the file folder to Frank.

The rundown was simple. Michael makes the hand off. Frank blindly pulls one page out of the stack that Michael hands him. Frank then reads that page, and that page only.

Michael waited patiently as Frank's eyes scanned the page, left to right and top to bottom. These were tense moments, as Michael studied Frank's face for the slightest tell in his facial expression. Unfortunately, Frank had one hell of a poker face.

Frank finished the page he had chosen, reinserted it into the stack, and set them down on the table. The usual scenario played out that if Frank didn't like the page, he would motion for the check. If he did like the page, he would call the server over for another round of drinks.

Frank raised his hand and the server came walking over. Michael waited to hear the request.

"I'll take the check now, please," Frank spoke sternly to the server.

Michael's heart sank. Another rejection. This one makes six in the last year.

Frank saw the expression on Michael's face.

"I know this isn't the way we normally do things, but I really have to be going. I have to make five more appointments before the day is over. But, Michael, I enjoyed it."

A ray of hope struck Michael's face.

"Oh," he was stunned. "So, what does this mean?"

"This means that I have one hell of a busy week. And now, I have to squeeze in reading the first four chapters of your new project."

The two shook hands as Frank flashed Michael a promising smile.

"Well, that sounds great Frank. I really appreciate it."

"This is a good start, Michael. This is good writing, but it's not great."

"Okay," Michael always took criticism poorly. "I understand."

"Now, I've only begun. The important thing is that we have something we can work with. Leave the pages with me, and I will read them and bring you feedback in a few days. Meanwhile, you keep writing."

"Thanks so much, Frank. I really appreciate it."

Frank stood from the table, collecting his credit card from the bill, and added another firm handshake before heading out of the bar.

Part Four

Michael was in no way, shape, or form an experienced drinker. In fact, he often thought it a terrible stereotype that all writers were just drunk storytellers. But on days like today, days when it was all good news, Michael had a reason to celebrate.

He was already in the bar, and so over the course of a few hours, several gin and tonics had come and gone.

Michael sat contemplating the incredible amount of work he had poured into the last few years, desperately trying to recreate the success of his first novel. As the drinks kept coming, the bar began to slowly fill as the afternoon turned into evening.

The jukebox volume was slowly increasing, and by the time Michael realized how much time he had actually spent in the bar, the place was packed and the jukebox was screaming out some Rolling Stones.

He stood from the table to make a trip to the bathroom. He stumbled through the crowd and finally found his way. Making his way back to his table, someone grabbed his arm. It was a fresh-faced young woman.

"Um, excuse me, but aren't you Michael Walker?"

He was puzzled as to how this woman recognized him. The picture from the jacket of his successful book was quite different than his current appearance.

"Uh, yes, ma'am. I am Michael Walker."

"I told you guys!" she exclaimed turning to the table full of what Michael assumed was college age kids. "I asked the bartender. He said he knew you and that you were Michael Walker. I looooved your book!"

Michael's eyes focused on her face. She was quite pretty: her big brown eyes, dark hair and a very petite body. Michael stared for a beat too long at said body, and he refocused on her face, having caught himself staring.

"Oh, uh, thanks. I really appreciate it."

"My Lit professor said he thought you still lived in the city. This is so crazy, seeing you here, I mean," her enthusiasm drew Michael in.

Even in the time immediately after his book being published, Michael had never experienced such admiration. He felt almost like a rock star, as if Mick Jagger himself was singing to Michael through the jukebox. 'Satisfaction' was playing. Michael felt himself wanting to explore this feeling more and more.

"I have a table over there if you wanted to join me," he smiled wryly at her. The alcohol had completely taken over his body and mind at this point. Never had Michael been a forward person in these situations, in fact he could not really remember having ever been in this situation.

"Oh, uh," the girl scanned her friends' faces for some type of guidance, whether it be approval or not. "Okay!"

She hopped up from the table, grabbed her drink and stood attentively waiting for Michael to lead the way back to his table.

The crowd had grown even larger during their brief exchange, and she reached out for his hand once he began walking.

"It's crazy in here, I don't want to lose you," she called out.

A smile came over Michael's face. He felt pride, a great pride; a "strength-of-ten-men" pride. He led her over to his table and they sat.

"So, what's your name?"

"I'm Mandy. I'm a junior, studying English Lit. It's so crazy to be sitting here talking with you!"

"Well, thanks. I appreciate it. Um..." he was growing more and more bashful. "So, English Lit? Do you want to teach?"

"That's the plan. I mean, I have done a lot of creative writing, but I would love to teach some day. I had some amazing teachers over the years, but I have never had one that really made literature fun, ya know?"

"Sure," Michael felt her drawing closer and closer to him with each question. "That was always a problem for me, too. I would have teachers that assigned reading lists, but for kids that didn't already love to read, there was no motivation."

"I agree completely," Mandy gazed at him as if he was Mick Jagger singing to her. Michael was feeling more and more confident. It was not his imagination either, as she slid down the bench of the booth towards him

Immediately, the sex chat line commercials came flooding into his head, and he began to look at Mandy differently.

"I'm working on a new book," he blurted. 'I'm sure Jagger used to tell girls about new albums all time' he thought to himself. He could feel his feathers spreading, as this gross display of peacocking grew more and more apparent.

She slid in until her thigh was touching his leg. She leaned in toward him and pursed her lips. She closed her eyes and went in for a kiss.

'It can't really be this easy' and 'Why has this never happened to me before?' simultaneously went through his head.

"Excuse me!" A deep voice pronounced from the edge of the table. Michael turned his attention to the man standing there, a mountain of a man. He was young, he was big, and he was angry.

"Tom!" Mandy cried out in a surprised voice. "Oh, no…"

The cab dropped Michael off outside of his building. He paid the driver and stepped out onto the street. He flung his blazer over his shoulder and stared down at the bloodstains on his white dress shirt.

Tom was Mandy's boyfriend. He was also a linebacker for the football team. Michael's intelligence couldn't quite persuade Tom to see his side of the story, and the two had tussled outside the bar in the alley.

Michael wasn't much of a fighter, and to top if off, Tom was. Luckily for Michael, his drunken state acted as a bit of a painkiller.

He stumbled to the door and stepped inside the building. He made his way for the elevator. Once inside, he examined his face in the stainless steel doors. His left eye was blackened, and his lip split on the right side.

It was only a short trip until he reached the seventh floor. As the doors opened, he could hear a bit of commotion down the hall toward his apartment. He drew closer and could make out the shape of a man standing at his door. The man was knocking and calling out Michael's name.

"Hey, Michael! Come on, man, open up!"

Once Michael could hear his voice, he stopped dead in his tracks. It was his oldest brother George. George was short and stocky, unlike Michael. In fact, to see the two out on the street, no one would peg them as brothers. He had thinning hair and a moustache. He kept banging on the door.

Michael stood frozen. Of all of his siblings, George was the only that Michael really feared. It was not real fear, as if to say George was a physical threat. It was fear fueled by their fathers' last words.

On his deathbed after the car accident, Michael's father made George promise that he would take over as the "man" of the family, that he would take care of his mother and always keep the others in line.

For George to be outside of Michael's apartment meant that something was either very wrong or that George was coming to straighten Michael out.

It wasn't long after Michael stepped out of the elevator that George noticed him in the hallway.

"Michael?"

"George," Michael answered his brother. His drunken haze clearing immediately as he felt the earnestness of the situation.

"Jesus Christ, Michael," George noticed the bruises and blood stained shirt. "What happened to you?"

"Just a little misunderstanding, George. No big deal."

"Sam said he was worried about you, but I had no idea."

"No idea what? I'm fine, George. Don't go flying off the handle. Why are you here? To lecture me?"

"Maybe I should Michael! Look at you, you're 29 years old coming in in the middle of the night with the crap kicked out of you! What is going on in your life?"

"George," Michael's frustration was growing. "I don't need this right now, man. You are obviously here for a reason. Just say it so I can go to work."

"Work? Work! You stumble in at 3 am stinking of gin and bloodied up, and now you're going to work?"

"Stop with the damn lectures, George! I don't want to hear it!"

"Fine! Fine!" George paced the hallway a bit, his short frame casting a large shadow.

Michael watched him, fuming from the implications and absurdity.

"Did you come out here to lecture me? Really, George?"

"You know, I wanted to come out here, sit down and have a conversation. I wanted to know my little brother was still alive. I wanted to know my little brother was happy with what he was doing. I didn't want to be greeted with this damn hostility! I call a dozen times on the way here, I'm sitting outside your place for hours, and this is what I see? What are you doing to yourself?"

Michael was absolutely fuming.

"George, I am really not in the mood for this right now. I had a bad night, and you come in here expecting the worst anyway, so yeah, why not see me like this!"

"Listen, when dad died..."

"Don't you dare! Don't you dare bring that up! George! Don't you dare…"

George lowered his head, realizing that the one thing he could say to anyone of his siblings to set them in line wasn't going to get through to Michael.

"Fine! You want to do it like this? Fine!!" George took a moment to catch his breath.

"Mom is sick. There, there you go. We had to do it like this?!"

Michael was stunned, stopped dead like a deer in headlights. He stepped back to lean up against the wall. His breathing became quick and short.

"Had to do it like this? We can't just be civil and discuss things!" George's anger spilling over, as Michael struggled to process what George just said.

"It's cancer, Michael. They think they found it early enough to save her, but it's not one hundred percent."

Michael couldn't speak, he stared down at his shoes, relying on the wall to hold up his weight. He struggled to breathe.

"You should probably come home soon and see her, just in case."

With that said, George turned and walked away from Michael, back down the hallway and into the elevator. The elevator doors closed and he was gone, just as quick as he had come.

Michael's knees buckled and he fell to the floor.

Michael was lost. Hunched on the floor outside of his apartment, the weight of what George had said sat on his chest. His breathing was heavy, and he couldn't fight back the tears. His mind busied itself, flashing through the past events of the last couple days: his little brother begging to spend time with him, a request he ignored, his run in with a pretty girl and her boyfriend, and the visions of Amy.

He was not the man his mother knew. He was not the man that Amy fell in love with. He was not the man his father knew.

That was where Michael got his knack for story telling, his father. As a child, Michael's father would always have big barbecues on Sundays, inviting the whole neighborhood into his backyard. Michael's father was known for always having a great story to tell. Instead of running and playing with the other children, Michael would sit there on one of the many ice chests while his father sat in a ring of middle-aged men all plopped down in lawn chairs. Some stories would go on for hours, and not a single person in that circle would speak. They were fixed on the man as he painted pictures of war and hardship, love and lust, and tall, tall tales.

In his early teenage years, Michael would sit at the kitchen table every night after the dinner table was cleared and his homework was done and scribble in an old notebook. When his brothers or sisters would come around, he would hover over the paper, hiding his words from them. But, when his mother would peek over his shoulder, he would proudly push the paper into better view.

"Just like your father," she would say as she rubbed his shoulders. She always had warm hands, and such a soothing voice.

Immediately, George's words came piercing through his memories. The differentiation of reality and fantasy was quickly coming, and warm memories of his mother became too painful to continue.

He stood, startled by the shock of clarity. He fumbled in his pocket for his keys. Just as he found them, he stopped. He looked at the door, visualizing what lay beyond them. It was no more a home as it was a dungeon; a small room where he spent all his time slaving away over a typewriter, and three other rooms left almost abandoned and cold.

He searched his mind for another place he could go. He had

no real friends to fall back on. The only numbers in his cell phone contact list were a cold-hearted businessman and a punk drug dealer. The rest were family, and he was guessing they would not be much comfort at this point.

He headed back for the elevator, deciding to head down to the diner on the corner to sit for a while. At least there would be other people around there. He knew he couldn't be alone.

Part Five

He grew more and more annoyed as he made his way down the street. His drunken stumbling was hailing every cab that passed. As they slowed down, he would angrily wave them away. The night was a fog of a light rain, blurred streetlights and a constant cloud of smoke rising from his mouth and into his eyes.

The diner glowed against the dark apartment buildings and empty shops that lined his street. He walked in and scanned the room to find a secluded booth where he could sulk in peace. He made his way down to the far end of the diner, just past the cash register, and settled into a booth in the corner.

Scuffling clangs came from the kitchen. The place was nearly empty, other than an older couple having coffee in a window booth. Michael focused on them as they sat silently. She meticulously forked away small pieces of her pie, positioning them perfectly before bringing them to her mouth. Meanwhile, he sipped a cup of coffee and read a newspaper.

Normally, Michael would be compiling back-story, having a full history of this couple within minutes. But tonight, his mind was a million different places. His imagination and curiosity were switched off. Instead, he observed this couple taking from them only a sense of comfort and normalcy.

A waitress interrupted his blank stare.

"Hey there, mister. What can I get for you?"

Michael's eyes broke from their stare and refocused on her face.

She looked tired. Her brown hair was pulled back but falling in several places. Her eyes sank into bags beneath them. Her short frame slumped forward, as if she had been on her feet for days on end. But, she was still smiling.

"Um," he fumbled for a menu. "I guess, just coffee?"

"Just coffee? Regular or decaf?"

Michael began to answer, but she interrupted.

"Actually we don't have decaf right now. If you want decaf, I can make some, but it'll be a few minutes."

She took a deep breath, as if just speaking was pushing her beyond her exhaustion.

"No, no. Regular please."

She turned and walked away, her feet shuffling low to the ground as if lifting them to take full steps was far beyond reasonable. Michael watched as she made her way back behind the counter and grabbed the coffee pot.

'Perspective?' he thought to himself, quickly rifling through assumptions of both her work and home life. Clearly, she was working for something, and pushing herself to far limits for a reason.

It wasn't long and she was back to the table with his coffee and a small dish filled with creamers.

"Thank you," he murmured.

"More than welcome. My name is Sarah. Just give me a call if you need anything else."

She turned away and shuffled back to the counter.

His eyes quickly turned back to the couple sitting at the window. The woman had finished her piece of pie, and was now just gazing out the window. The man thumbed through the paper still, but looked up now and again to glance at his wife.

Michael couldn't help but place his parents in that booth, old and gray, content. They always were, he remembered. They would sit out on the porch in the warm summer evenings, talking and periodically waving at people passing by on the street.

The town he grew up in was as small town as they come. Everyone knew everyone, and people did not pass each other with a kind hello.

He saw them sitting there, just like that old couple. Not

needing to speak, just needing to be sitting across from each other. But, his father was gone, and now, his mother was not far behind, or so it felt.

When Michael moved away to the city after his father passed, his mother was very angry with him. She would not speak to him, in fact a month before he left was the last time they spoke for almost a year. His sisters would plead with him to call her, but he was stubborn. He knew what she would say; he knew she would ask him to come home.

All five of his siblings at different points reached out to him to contact her. But, he never found the right way to deal with his father passing. He saw the man in his brother's faces, and couldn't face his mother without being reduced to tears.

As the old man across the diner from him read, occasionally his mouth would turn up just a bit, a stern form of smiling. Whether it was a good story or just a good line in the article he was reading, his stone face would slightly turn soft for a moment. This reminded Michael a lot of his father.

Right out of high school, Michael struggled with the decision of college: where to go and what to study. He entered a handful of writing competitions in the meantime. He ended up winning one of those contests; the prize including a cash prize as well as a trip to New York City for a reading at the public library in front of the press and the public. His parents threw Michael a big party the day he returned. Most of the town had turned out at their house, as this was the first time anyone from their small community had made national news.

The party was a parade of people passing by, shaking Michael's hand and congratulating him. The one thing that Michael always remembered about that party was that the entire day, his father stood there by his side as he spoke to everyone in the neighborhood. He listened proudly as Michael explained his accomplishment and his future plans of writing time and time again to each passerby. The look on his father's face all day was that of the old man reading the paper, a half smile slightly softening his normally hardened, gruff exterior.

As Michael's attention slid back to the woman gazing out the window onto the street, a vision of his mother came to him. Guilt washed over him. Not only had he broken contact with her, other than the sparse phone conversations on birthdays and major holidays, but with the news of her having cancer, his mind only focused on his father.

Having never completely dealt with the loss of his father, the news of his mother's sickness was like a beam of light on the dark place he hid those feelings of sorrow, anger, and confusion.

Michael remembered back to his childhood, the way his mother worked night and day to provide for six children. There were no breaks; there were no days off. And still, she was always so kind, so calm, and so understanding. Though Michael was not very involved in sports when he was growing up, his brothers and sisters were constantly in the midst of some type of team activity. And there his mother would be, for every game, every meet, every contest, cheering on her children. Resilience.

As he thought of his sisters, he could see those traits in them as well. The youngest, Lily, was an elementary school teacher and soon-to-be married. The middle sister, Rose, was a nurse. And the oldest of the three, Millie, was a social worker and mother of two. All of his sisters were pursuing careers in which the main focus was helping people.

He smiled as he took the last gulp from his coffee cup. Just as he set it back to the table, the waitress walked up with pot in hand. She poured him another cup, and asked if he needed anything else.

"Oh, no thank you. This will be fine," he said.

"Are you sure? Some food would probably help you sober up," she suggested.

He looked to her face, as she stood hand on hip and slightly hunched forward.

"I mean, I smelled it on you before you walked in the door."

"Yeah," he awkwardly answered. "Um, I'm good."

He looked to the nametag pinned to her uniform: Sarah.

"But, thanks, Sarah," he smiled at her.

She turned away to head back for the counter when she stopped and turned back.

"I feel like I recognize you. Where do I know you from?"

His first thought went immediately to his book jacket picture. Quickly realizing that his current appearance was nothing close to that, he paused: "Um, I'm not sure, really."

"If you don't mind me asking, are you from around here?"

"Yeah, I live just a block up. I'm in the York building on the corner."

"Wait, really? I live there too!" A look of shock came over her face, as if she thought she knew everyone in that building and his face wasn't familiar. "I'm in 7D."

"Huh, that's funny. I'm in 8D."

It took Michael a moment to put the puzzle together. This was the woman that lived below him, the mother of two that always disrupted his writing days.

Just as he realized, he could see in her face that she realized as well.

"Oh..." a smirk came to her face. "You're the writer?"

"Um, yeah, Michael," he extended his hand as if to greet her for the first time.

"8D, huh," she mumbled as she took his hand in hers.

Michael could feel the almost immediate wave of hostility emanating from her.

"You are the guy that complained to the super that my kids are too loud," she scoffed.

"Oh, yeah, sorry about that. I have an odd schedule when I'm working and..." he was interrupted mid-sentence.

"At six o'clock at night, you complain about the noise. 6

p.m."

"Yeah," he hung his head, a sense of shame as her point hit home. He was an adult man complaining about children in the middle of the evening, after all.

"Well, I hope we have been more compliant, I'm trying to keep it down."

"No, no. I'm sorry it's really no bother. In fact, I see how ridiculous it all is," he backtracked, trying to calm the frustration he could read in her eyes. He quickly searched his mind for something to say to break the tension.

"Oh, uh, working the late shift, huh? Is your husband watching the kids?"

Her hostility turned to hurt, as if her heart sank from her chest to her stomach.

"Uh, no. I'm not married," she began. Michael closed his eyes, realizing that what he chose to say was not the right thing at all. "My neighbor, Mrs. Johnson, watches the boys when I have to work the graveyard. Ya know, it's nice to have good neighbors."

He felt her jabbing him with that comment.

"So, what's your story, then? I mean, I thought I knew everyone in that building."

"Oh," Michael began. He took a second to choose his words carefully, having already put his foot in his mouth more than once. "I am a writer, as you know. I don't really get out much when I'm working, which is probably why we don't know each other."

She stood there. The diner now empty with the departure of the elderly couple from the window booth, she was waiting to hear more.

"I had a book a few years back do pretty well, so now I'm trying to repeat that success." He scanned her face for approval.

"So you are writing one now?" she asked, her voice slightly losing the edge it previously had.

"Yeah, I'm working now." He was uncomfortable with the direction of the conversation, as he never spoke in detail about projects he was working on. He looked to her, searching for a path to lead the conversation down without offending her again.

"So, what gets you out of the apartment, then? Out on the town?" she asked.

"Kind of, I guess. I had a good meeting with my editor, so I guess I was celebrating."

"Well the shiner and fat lip suggest otherwise." She made a fist and playfully mimicked punching him.

Michael took a moment. "It was pretty crazy of me to complain about the noise. I get pretty wrapped up in what I'm doing and don't really think about anyone else."

"Hey, I guess we all have our crosses, huh?"

"Yeah. I guess."

Just as Michael was redeeming himself in the conversation, the bell over the door rang and a group of four piled in from the street.

"Well, let me know if you need anything then, Michael," as she turned away to greet the new customers.

Michael sat for a bit, a quiet calm falling on him. His eyes no longer blurred the coffee cup in his hands as he rose it to his mouth for another drink. He looked over to Sarah as she busily made the new customers their drinks.

The scope of the world that he lived in for the past year was so incredibly narrow. Now, as the world beyond that scope came plunging in with the bad news of his mother's illness and the chance meeting with the woman he complained about almost daily, he realized that his scope needed to be widened, and by great lengths.

The morning came calling in the form of the telephone ringing. Waking from a slumped position on his couch, Michael took a moment to register his surroundings. The hi-fi skipped, having found the end of the album long ago. The room was filled with the light of day, and an ashtray full of cigarette butts overflowed onto the coffee table.

Again, the ringing came from the kitchen. He stood to answer it, the echoes in his head deafening as he walked.

"Hello," he answered gruffly as he reached the kitchen and grabbed the receiver from the wall.

"Michael? I'm glad I caught you," Michael recognized the voice as Frank.

"Oh, hey, Frank."

"Good news, Michael. I got a meeting with the publishers this afternoon. I'm ready to start moving on this new project."

The news took a second to set in. Less than twenty-four hours had passed since Frank first saw the pages.

"Oh, wow, that's great," Michael answered.

"When I finally got a chance to sit down last night, I started reading more pages. I couldn't put it down. This is much better than I anticipated. How soon until you can get me more pages?"

"Wow, well…" Michael took a moment to calculate in his mind. Normally, when working constantly, Michael could churn out a novel in just weeks. "I have five more chapters finished that you don't have, and I assume another six or seven to finish. Maybe, a week or so?"

"Okay," Frank answered abruptly. "Well, get to work then. I plan on pitching this thing today if they'll let me. Otherwise, I'll try and schedule a pitch within the next few days."

Michael smiled. A weight lifted off his shoulders, and a deep sigh of relief poured from his lips. He had only heard Frank so enthusiastic about a project once before: his first novel.

"Well, that sounds great Frank. I'll get to work immediately. Thanks a lot."

"I'll be in touch. If they take the pitch today, you'll be hearing from me tonight. Regardless, I'll need the other chapters as soon as possible."

"Okay, thanks Frank."

As he hung up the phone, Michael slumped back against the wall. It had been years since he felt such a calm wash over him. He immediately reached to his shirt pocket and pulled a cigarette from the pack. Placing it between his lips and lighting it, he turned to the coffee pot and assembled a filter ready for brewing.

With the coffee started, he walked to the bathroom. He flipped the light and examined himself in the mirror: a fat lip, a black eye, blood stains on his shirt, and an old red tie loosened about his neck. He smiled as he took another drag from his cigarette.

When he was working, Michael always maintained a very short-term memory. Had he made a complete fool of himself at the bar last night? Yes. Had he made an ass of himself with the waitress? Yes. Did he have an emotional breakdown after speaking with his brother George? Yes.

But all that was gone now. Now, he was working on a novel set for publishing.

Part Six

He sat at the typewriter, rolling it back to reread the last few lines to refresh his mind of where he had left off. Once confident he was back in the thick of it, his fingers went to keys. He typed away vigorously. Page after page was added to the stack neatly sitting beside the typewriter.

Hours passed with him only taking a second to strike up another cigarette or trudge down the hall to refill his coffee cup. His fingers, though cramping slightly, still pecked away ferociously.

Upon finishing a page, he took a moment to stretch, leaning back in his desk chair. He looked to the window, and the slight sliver of the real world beyond that heavy blanket that cloaked the frame. A soft orange light was coming in, and he assumed the sun was setting.

He stood to walk back down the hallway once more. As he reached the kitchen, he noticed the clock on the microwave: 5:15. As he poured himself another cup of coffee, he thought of Sarah. Soon she would be getting off work and the noise from below would begin.

He could see her: that white uniform, her hair disheveled and strewn about, groceries in one arm, a child in the other with the second boy following close behind. She would struggle just to get her keys from her purse to open her apartment door. Once inside, she would juggle making dinner and giving her boys, having spent the day with her elderly neighbor, the attention they wanted from her.

As hard as he worked, as much as he put into his writing, Michael was certain he had never known a day in his life as challenging as everyday for her.

He lingered for a moment there at the coffee pot, leaning against the kitchen counter, laughing as he noticed that he was still wearing the bloodstained shirt from the night before. He shook is head, recalling in his mind the conversation that he had had with Sarah the night before. She was so angry with him for having complained about the noise her boys made in the evenings when she finally got them home. She had every right to be angry; his complaints simple, selfish requests for everything around him to be still and quiet so he could work.

Even though she was clearly agitated with their chance meeting, when he began speaking of his writing, she lost the edge and attitude and seemed to listen. Perhaps she was just taking some sort of pity on him in his drunken, beaten state. Clearly, in her eyes, he seemed to be a complete mess of a man; a selfish, arrogant asshole writing his stories and not having to deal with the reality that was her everyday life.

As he sipped at his mug, he heard the slam of the door beneath them. They were home. He snapped out of his mind for a moment, just long enough to look to the microwave clock again. A half hour had passed since he came into the kitchen.

'Wow, get back to work' he thought to himself. He scolded himself for allowing his mind to wander off topic for long enough to waste a half of an hour. After all, he was on a deadline now. 'Not a moment to waste'.

Not long after, the hi-fi was blaring an old Dylan record and he sat comfortably on his couch; Dylan's harsh voice stinging poignant lyrics through the haze that filled the living room, the blue light of the television giving everything a soft glow.

Michael was contemplating the ending. This was a big moment. He never came to the ending until he was absolutely certain he knew how the entire story would play out. Just in the day's work, he had completed two full chapters, and begun on a third. He was confident he knew where the story was going, where it had been, and now he was working on the ending.

His heroine awoke with the morning's first light. Brushing the hair from her eyes, she smiled. It was her wedding day. Years had passed since the story's beginning, and she stood in front of a full-length mirror closely examining the woman staring back at her. She had overcome all the adversities in her life, and finally found the man that would take her hand forever.

She had Amy's eyes. She had Amy's smile. She watched as she slowly pulled a brush through her long blonde hair, just as Amy used to do. She stood there in a long white dress, soft against her porcelain skin.

The string quartet struck up and the people seated neatly in rows along a long aisle stood and turned to see her. She began walking slowly, arm in arm with her father. He looked at her, tears in his eyes and clutching her hand as it rest in his. She studied the faces as she passed them, each one looking at her exactly as she imagined they would. They lingered in her beauty, and they longed for the happiness that her smile projected.

As she drew closer to the altar, her eyes focused on the man waiting for her at the end. Positioned next to the preacher, he stood tall and solid in a black tuxedo and white bowtie. With each step her eyes focused more and more on his face. The tears began to well in her eyes as she passed her mother.

Her father stopped at the end of the aisle, lifting her veil to kiss her on the cheek, tears now flowing consistently down his face. "I love you so much, pookie," he whispered. He had called her 'Pookie' her entire life. Her earliest memory was that of him bouncing her on his knee and smiling as she giggled, the tight curls on her head bouncing in rhythm. He then stepped to the man in the tuxedo and extended his hand.

"You take care of her, now. That's my baby girl."

The man shook her father's hand and answered, "Yes, sir. With everything I have."

As her father turned to join her mother, her eyes fixed on the man standing before her. He stepped in close to her and lifter her veil.

As her eyes focused through the tears, she could see his

face. It was a very familiar face. It was Michael's face.

Michael's eyes jolted open. They took a moment to focus, with only the blue light from the television registering. His palms were sweaty and his pulse racing. As he struggled to catch his breath, he sat upright on the couch, coughing on the way up.

Once composed, he glanced back to microwave clock: 7:45 pm. He grabbed his pack of cigarettes from the coffee table and jumped up from his seat. He made his way down the hall to his office, taking his seat at the typewriter.

The hum of the streetlamps was now the only sound filling the office. Michael sat hunched over his typewriter, head in hands. Smoke poured from a cigarette stuck between two fingers. The small ring of light from his desk lamp shone on the paper in the typewriter.

'Damnit' he thought. He pulled the paper from its home and crumpled it in his hands. He threw the ball of paper to the corner of the room, making a light thud as it crashed against the others. He grabbed the light and shown it at the corner he had been littering with rejects, only to discover a small mountain beginning to form.

He stood from his desk, pushing the chair back with his legs, and stepped away. Grabbing his coffee cup from its seat, he turned and headed down the hallway for the kitchen. The microwave read three o'clock.

Frustration had long since set in. He had been so certain when he sat back at the typewriter that he had it all figured out. Somewhere between here and there, something had gone completely wrong: his words were flat and short, his descriptions were dull and misconstrued.

A long sigh and he reached for another cigarette. Hours had passed since any progress had come from his hands. Normally, his mind was so focused when he was working, but now, he was struggling to focus on anything.

His mother pushed herself to the forefront. All he could

see was her now. He stood there in the kitchen, puffing on his cigarette, and imagining his mother lying in a hospital bed. The last time Michael saw his mother was more than eight months ago when he made a short trip home for Christmas. He searched his memory for any indication that she looked anything other normal. He found nothing; she looked fine. She looked happy, in fact. She was pouring over her grandchildren, she was joking with her sons, and she was baking with her daughters.

"I wish you'd visit more," he remembered her saying.

"It's complicated, Ma," is all he said in reply. It was all he ever said.

Previously, when Michael would think of his mother, the memory that came to him was that of the summer following his father's death. He had made a trip home to attend his grandmother's funeral. She had spent the last few years of her life in a nursing home, and it came as no surprise to the family when she passed. It was a much different feeling at her funeral than at his father's funeral. Though no one wanted to admit it, it was a lot easier. She had lived a very long life, and though sad, his family spent more time remembering her than missing her that day.

But he always remembered what his mother said to them all that day. For a long time after his father passed, there was seldom a conversation that Michael had with his mother that shed any positive light on what life was or was supposed to be. But that day, standing there in her home, in front of all of her extended family, his mother smiled and spoke sternly: "I hope we all get to stay as long as she did. And I hope we all get to see as much as she did."

It was not some dramatic, Shakespearean monologue. It was simple. But for the first time since her husband's passing, all those members of her family saw that she was okay, that she was coping. That's the image that Michael always reverted to when he thought of his mother.

Now, it had changed. Now it was sad. He didn't want to

think of her sick, in a hospital, weak and dejected. Michael had no experience with cancer, he knew only the stereotypical things: the bandanas to cover baldheads, the weakness and constant vomiting chemotherapy caused, and yes, death.

The microwave rang out as the processed frozen dinner inside finished cooking. Michael snapped back into reality. He pulled it from inside, his fingertips burning from the cheap, plastic plate holding his food.

"It's complicated, Ma," kept ringing in his ears.

As he walked to the couch to sit and eat, he glanced down the hall to the office, the desk lamp's focus still shooting against the stack of wadded papers in the corner. For the first time since he began this recent project, that was the last place Michael wanted to be.

Part Seven

He would never come out and admit it, his distain for people that is. It was never really this way. Growing up, he truly enjoyed being around his family, and though shy, was quite eager to meet new people. It wasn't until he had really sunk his teeth into writing that he began to separate himself from others. The career path he chose was not an easy one, and he knew that from the beginning. He worked day and night, in as concentrated a rhythm as possible. Other than his family and his relationship with Amy, Michael completely cut himself off from other people. After losing his father, the family ties became strained, as he fought to deal with his loss. Amy was all he had, and he never really allowed her in any more than he had to.

It was a theory he developed after his father's passing and the impending doom that was his breakup with Amy. He saw two kinds of people in this world: "happy" people and "working" people. "Happy" people lived their lives in circles, repetitions, and routines. They lived simple lives: married, kids, good job that pays the bills but doesn't demand much effort, and a structure of family and friends that they surrounded themselves with. "Working" people were driven individuals; creative people, intellectual people, the real go-getters of the world.

Michael saw himself as a "working" person. He devoted himself completely to his writing. He also loathed "happy" people. "Happy" people were not risk takers, they never invested too heavily in things; thus, the idea of 'one door closes, another one opens' came about. If they lost a job, they would just find another one. If a car broke down, they would just take out another loan and get a new one. They were always in position to fall and be able to pick themselves back up.

However, Michael saw this as weakness. Boring, completely and utterly boring. The pattern would simply work itself out, completing the circle of the "happy" life: a never-ending drone of monotony in which mediocrity is not only mistaken for elation, but also the goal.

This theory rang on and on in his ears as he sit in front of the blue light of a predawn infomercial flashing from the television screen. He was still dreadfully blocked, now going on three separate sessions in which he achieved nothing; three separate occasions over the course of twenty-four hours where he sat at the typewriter and forced himself to write something. The only result of those sessions was that the mountain of throwaway pages had doubled.

There was no fall back plan. It was writing or nothing. It was as if this story and the interest that it had peaked in Frank was the rope tied in a noose. Michael chose to tie the noose, and he always chose to slip his head in; complete and utter devotion. There was no other door that could open. If this project failed, that chair would be kicked out from under him and he would go down with it, legs kicking and flailing.

Michael was not and could never see himself being a "happy" person. He ate, drank, and slept writing. This story was the only air he breathed. It was not his job; there was no eight hour day and then it's home to the wife and kids for dinner or out to the bar with the boys to catch a game. It was complete and utter surrender to plot and dialogue, to protagonists and conflict. It was isolation.

That made it worse when he was blocked. Suddenly, he was frantic. His mind raced for the answer, yet at the same time, every idea that came was under absurd scrutiny. He began questioning everything, as if he was back in the beginning. Was he not structuring the sentences correctly? Did he miss something along the way that would hinge the entire story? Is the plot even the same from beginning to end?

There was no element of the story that was safe from this watchtower of doubt. It was as if his every move was wrong. 'Why are you sitting here on the couch? Get in there and get through this?' teetered with 'Don't go back in there! You're only going to frustrate yourself even more!'

Occasionally, he would glance over his shoulder to the kitchen and peer in at the telephone. He knew the call was coming. He knew Frank would completely steam roll the executives at the publishing house, and that Frank would be calling demanding the rest of the pages to be compiled for the rough draft.

Years he had waited. Years for an idea to sit up enough to get the attention it needed to get picked up. Now, he sat on the brink of a single phone call that could redirect his career, and he couldn't finish the story. He wouldn't have the pages when Frank came calling for them.

He sat there in his living room; mindless jargon on the television, three packs worth of cigarette butts in the ashtray and on the coffee table. A quarter lay there on the table next to the ashtray. All over the face of the table, there were perfect circles dug through the finish, and bare wood was exposed. He had been pressing on the coin with his thumb, grinding it into the table; a stress-relief habit of his.

He truly felt as if his mind was letting him down. The minutes ticked away, and that phone call was coming whether the pages were written or not.

And there it was, as he woke in a start. He sat up from the couch, where he had fallen asleep hunched into his usual spot. Wiping drool from his cheek, he sprung up from the couch. From the kitchen came that fateful ring, and it rang again.

He hurried to answer it.

"Hello?" he spoke nervously.

"Michael?"

A brief sigh came over him as he recognized the voice as his brother Sam.

"Sam," he answered. "Hey."

"Hey, Michael, listen I uh…" Sam always stuttered a bit

when his nerves were getting the best of him. "I talked to George and…"

Michael interrupted his brother. "Sam, come on man. I have a lot going on right now."

"Yeah, yeah, we all know Mike. We all know how busy you are. That's great, I guess, that you're busy. That's really great."

Sam waited a beat, allowing his sarcasm to sink in. When Michael didn't answer, Sam spoke again.

"Listen, I am a faithful man, Michael. I really am. And I really feel that the relationship between you and I is some kind of test for me, some kind of lesson on patience or something. I have to be honest with you, right now, I really could care less."

Michael listened as his little brother spoke firmly.

"It's not about you anymore, Michael; not with me, not with George, not with anybody. It's not about you. It's about Mom."

Michael took a deep breath. His mind was completely taxed and his body was tired. He didn't have the energy to interject.

"George said you know. She's really sick, really sick." There was a pause before he continued. "She has been asking about you a lot lately."

"Sam…"

The younger of the two didn't even allow his brother to speak.

"I'm not telling you to come home. I'm just telling you that your sick mother has been asking about you."

The phone went dead. Michael held the receiver out away from his ear, as if he was shocked his brother had hung up on him.

As he hung up the phone, his brother's words were sinking in. For so long, he had blazed his path as far away from home as possible. So much so now that it appeared as if his siblings had completely given up on him, not to blame them. Any effort to be anything resembling family was all on the part of them, not him.

A calendar hung on the side of the refrigerator. He took a second look to it, only to realize it had been months since he flipped the pages to stay current. As he thumbed the pages to get to present day, he was searching the dates to begin considering making a trip back to see his mother.

As he ran his finger along the days, the telephone rang again.

Michael stared at, wondering which of his other siblings was calling now.

Reluctantly, he reached out and answered it.

"Hello?"

"Michael, hey, it's Frank. Good news, the execs loved the pitch!"

It was morning, and Frank had just given a successful pitch. There was no greater time for a savvy businessman. His day was just starting and he was already counting his cut of the publishing deal.

"Oh, that's great, Frank," Michael answered, still a bit withdrawn from his previous conversation.

"Whoa, whoa, Michael. What's this I am hearing in your voice? How are you not more excited than me right now?"

"Oh, it's nothing Frank. No worries," Michael was always awful at backtracking. "So they loved it?"

"Eating out of my hand, Michael. They are excited to get a hold of the first draft by the end of the week. How are we looking, time wise?"

"Well, I have to be honest here, Frank. I haven't made any progress in days. I'm working on it though, I promise. Just a little jammed up," Michael hated apologizing. Frank came to expect a very high level of productivity from him based on past experiences. Now, Michael was the one delaying things.

"What's the problem? I have never known you to get blocked? You're not blocked, are you?" Frank's voice never got to the distress point in which one could determine he was worried, but this was probably the closest Michael had ever heard.

"No, blocked is a very harsh word, Frank. Progress has slowed, but I'm not blocked."

"Okay, that's good to know. I mean, not really, but slow is difficult but doable. Blocked is not doable. When can I expect more pages?"

"I'm working, Frank. I don't really want to promise pages," Michael became firmer.

"Well, Michael. I pitched this book because you told me we were close. Now, you are struggling? Be straight with me, Michael. Because I will not be made a fool of!"

"I got some personal stuff going on Frank. I'm not trying to make you look like a fool. I'm trying to focus. So, give me a little time and I will get you your pages."

"I'll be in touch, soon," Frank spouted off.

The basement of the apartment building doubled as storage space and a small garage. Though there was a sizeable parking lot behind the building itself, a handful of tenants chose to pay for a spot keep their nice cars out of the elements. There were BMWs, a few Lexus', and even a small foreign sports car that Michael couldn't pronounce the name of.

And then, there was his car. He stood before it puffing busily on a cigarette. It was a heap compared to the expensive vehicles surrounding it: an old gray Oldsmobile sedan, rust spots forming on the hood just above the headlights from where he had hit a deer years ago. From his place in the front of the car, Michael could see the tears in the leather seating, with dull yellow foam poking through. Another puff from his cigarette, and he moved around to the driver side door. He unlocked the door, popped it open and slid down inside.

He paid for the spot to keep the rust on the hood from getting worse faster, but he also paid for it to keep it out of the way of everyone else; people that actually drove their cars to get to jobs or take their kids to school.

Michael turned the car over, firing it up. He hadn't driven the car in months, but occasionally came down to start it up and keep everything in running order. Primarily, he kept this car to make trips back home. It had been a while since that trip was made, and he kind of figured that any time he tried to turn that key, it could be the last.

As he flipped through the programmed radio stations, he thought about the situation he found himself in. He was under fire for more pages, a task he longed for for the past few years. Yet, every time he sat at the typewriter, his frustration would only grow and the pages would not come. He was also under fire to return home and see his mother, his sick mother. For days, he had been weighing the pros and cons of the trip. His brothers and sisters had probably all but written him off, but he knew his mother had been asking for him.

If he left, he knew there would be hell to pay when Frank found out. Since the first day that Michael met Frank, he learned the extremes that Frank went to to promote his projects to get the publishers to sign on. He also knew that all Frank expected in return was finished projects worth his time. If Michael left town now, he knew it could possibly mean losing the deal with Frank.

He knew it was not a healthy relationship that he had with Frank. Not on a personal level, for they had very little of that. Frank was all business. When business was good, Frank was the nicest guy in the world. In fact, Michael had made the mistake after his first published book of thinking that Frank was his friend. He quickly learned the frailty of their relationship when Frank shot down his next project idea within mere seconds of reading a page. Quickly, Michael began to see Frank as the decider. If he would bring Frank an idea, that was either the jumping off point or the sudden death of it. Frank would sit there with his expensive suits and silk ties and sip his gin and tonic, and he would pass judgment, more often than not completely condemning an idea.

It wasn't fear. It was more of a nervous energy. Michael knew if he decided to leave town, he would not call Frank and explain himself. He would just go, typewriter in tow, and hope that perhaps the words would come to him while visiting his mother.

Maybe it was fear.

He turned the car off and stepped out of it. Closing the door and locking it, he pulled another cigarette from his shirt pocket. He stood there a minute, as the fantasy of just jumping in his car and driving off into the sunset played out in his head. He was never one to run from conflict, but it was day three of the block, and he was willing to do anything to get away from it.

Part Eight

The street was busy as people rushed to get home. The sun was setting and falling behind the apartment buildings. It was too early for the streetlamps to kick on, and his shadow stretched out far in front of him as he made his way down to the diner on the corner. The place he called his "refuge" for so long had quickly turned into a war zone. The apartment was cold and unwarranting of any productivity.

The bell rang out as he stepped inside. The place was packed. He shrugged as he realized his absolute distain for busy public places. Annoyed, he found himself the last seat open at the long counter that faced the kitchen. A bright-eyed girl popped up in front of him presenting a menu.

"Here ya go, sir," she squeaked as he she passed the menu over to him.

He wasn't even hungry, he just needed to get out of the apartment. Perhaps if he wasn't a chain smoker, he would have enjoyed a walk around the neighborhood. But, for Michael the trek down to the diner on the corner had taken it's toll on him.

The waitress' eyes roamed, bouncing around the busy room. She waited for a response, but quickly interjected: "Coffee?"

"Yeah, coffee..." he answered.

Mere seconds passed and she had the coffee in front of him with a small bowl of creamers. As she sped away to take care of her other customers, Michael turned a bit to scan the room. He was hoping to see Sarah.

Turning back to his coffee, his mind continued to race, as it always did. His frustration was reaching its peak. The longer he went without continuing the story, the more his personal worries crept into his head. It was a constant stream of his mother, his father, his brothers and sisters. He wondered how awful it would be to make the trip back home, how uncomfortable he would be having to explain himself to his siblings; or worse yet, to not have to explain himself because they just didn't care anymore.

The pretty girl from the bar and her meathead boyfriend crossed his mind once in a while too. Not too often, just enough to remind him of the pitfalls of drinking and egomania.

Amy came and went as well, though not as much as she usually would. He still dreamt of her at night, standing there in his living room. She had been the predominant figure of his fantasy for a long time, until the news of his mother came along and jostled him back into some state of reality.

He had been thinking a lot of Sarah as well. The years he spent cursing her and her two boys for disrupting his day, and the complete ass he had made of himself here at the diner.

Just as he began thinking of her, the swinging doors leading to the kitchen swung forward and she came walking through. She held trays stacked three high full of coffee mugs fresh from the dishwasher. She was hurried and focused on the task, and she didn't notice Michael as she walked right past.

He wanted to say something to catch her attention. But, he let her walk by seeing the weight she was carrying. She continued to the end of the counter and began putting the mugs in neat stacks below.

She stood upright once they were all in their rows, hands on hips and stretching her back. Her hair was disheveled just as the night they spoke. Her face looked weary and her uniform was visibly dirty.

As she made her way back down the counter, she passed Michael again; again not noticing him.

This time he spoke up. "Sarah?"

She stopped to allow her eyes to focus on the row of faces where she heard her name called from. She saw him there, hair messy and strewn about and beard unkempt and shaggy.

"Michael? Hey there," she answered him.

He smiled a bit, happy to see her.

"What brings you out this evening? Taking a break?" she asked.

"Shouldn't I ask you the same thing?" he replied, nodding toward the clock hung on the wall behind her.

"Yeah," she answered whipping around to see the time. "I'm pulling a double, a few gals couldn't make their shifts, so..."

"I see."

She stared at the coffee cup sitting in front of him. "Don't you ever eat?" she questioned.

"Oh," was all he said in return. He was enjoying the bit of banter they were sharing. Remembering how terribly their last conversation started, he was relieved that they picked up where they had left off.

"Ya know, Sammy made some really great soup today. How would you like a bowl? Baked potato?"

"Sure," he answered. With a smile, she turned and headed back for the kitchen.

As Michael sat back on his stool, he caught a glimpse of himself in the mirrors that lined the sections of the wall not left open to expose the kitchen. He was smiling. He also noticed how completely unmaintained he looked. He laughed to himself as he pulled on his beard to smooth it out, and combed his hair to the side with his fingers.

He could feel the wheels in his head slowing, the churning of a million thoughts lessening. Slowly his ears were unplugging from his own mind, and the clamor of the busy diner began slipping in. To his left, a couple was arguing about color palettes for a bed spread, the husband wanting to get the colors set so the trip to the department store would be quick and decisive. To his right, a man murmured under his breath, unconsciously reading the article from today's newspaper aloud. Michael laughed to himself, realizing he very well could do that same thing in public without even knowing.

Sarah was back in just a few minutes, placing the bowl of soup in front of Michael.

"Sammy's Special. Some say it's the best in the city, ya know."

"You don't say," he answered. "My little brother's name is Sam. Small world."

"Small world in deed. You should bring him by sometime and introduce me," Sarah spoke wryly. She smiled as she suggested the setup.

Michael smirked. "Yeah. He comes to town a few times a year for business."

"Well, there you go. I mean, don't mention the kids, that always scares the good ones away."

She was in surprisingly good spirits considering she was entering the second leg of her double shift.

"I'm sure he wouldn't mind. He's a good guy, that one."

Michael spoke of his brother with pride. Sam was a good guy: great job, smart, funny as hell. At least, that's the Sam that Michael knew a few years back, before Michael pulled away from all of them.

"It's pretty busy in here, so I need to make the rounds. But, I'll be back by to check on you."

She quickly turned away and busied herself amongst her many customers.

Michael ate the soup, and thought more of Sam. For all Michael knew, Sam could have changed, could be a completely different person now. He didn't know. And what of the others, all living a life that Michael knew nothing about.

As Sarah passed by on her way back to the kitchen, she flashed Michael a smile. There she was: a jilted mother of two working double shifts and overnight shifts, relying on an elderly neighbor to watch her kids, just to get by. And she was warm. She was kind. She had every reason to hate him; this monster of a man so lost inside his own head that he would complain about children making noise in the middle of the day. And yet, she was smiling at him, as her feet ached from standing all day and taking orders from people. She was smiling at him.

Just as he was finishing his soup, she was standing in front of him again.

"Did you like it?" she asked.

"Yeah. I did," he smiled at her as he spoke.

"Well, good to hear." She pulled the bowl from in front of him. He expected her to turn away, but she asked again: "Do you get to see your brother a lot, then? Him living out of town and all?"

"No, actually. I haven't seem him since Christmas. Any of them, actually."

"Them? How many brothers do you have?"

"Well, there's six of us, three sisters and two brothers."

"And you don't get to see any of them?" Her face was puzzled.

"They all live back home, in a little town a few hours away."

"Wow, let me just say that I would go crazy not seeing my family. I mean, all I have is my one sister; but between her and my parents, I don't know what I would do without them."

The look on her face wasn't pity, but it was close.

"I mean," her eyes grew big as she tried to fathom the idea. "They have always been there to help me out."

Michael studied her as she went from playful to serious in an instant. His eyes locked with hers.

And then she spoke sternly: "Family is everything."

If he was completely honest, weather never played a whole lot in Michael's life. Weather was the little thing he had to worry about when he needed to run down to the market for coffee and cigarettes.

It was August, and normally hot days cooled off in the evenings, making perfect conditions for rolling the windows down and blaring the radio. Michael enjoyed driving. It was a time when he could just be completely free, at least for the length of the trip.

In this case, it was three hours from the city to his hometown. Three hours of pavement and music. The moment he sat down behind the steering wheel, all the worries of his brothers' and sisters' reactions to him showing up faded away; along with the worries of what Frank would say.

Something about his conversation with Sarah really made sense. He had lost sight of the importance of a lot of things over the course of the past few years. He had thrown the idea of family away shortly after his father passed. Then, when he and Amy split, he had no real need for any outside influences that weren't in relation to his career.

It made him sick to his stomach to think that he debated the question of whether or not to go and see his mother. 'What's a few days? Frank is going to have to wait!' He was bold when he was driving. In truth, an awful lot of his epiphanies and revelations came while making this drive alone. When he first moved to the city, his revelation was: "I can do this on my own." It was the same thought when Amy left him.

There was only one order of business on these drives: arranging the accommodations. There were no hotels within thirty miles of his mother's house, and with the tense situation with his family members, Michael started spending his visits back staying with an old friend of his from high school: Jack.

The telephone rang about five times before Jack answered, always. He was a musician by choice, electrician by trade. His evenings were spent lounging around the basement, watching old bootlegged concerts on DVD and jamming along. He would sit in a beanbag chair while he did it, so it took the first three rings of the telephone just for him to get up and out of the chair.

"Jack's House of Rock," he answered. He always answered the phone this way. Michael wasn't sure if it was because he thought it was clever or witty, or if he just was still stuck in the high that was his glory days.

"Hey, Jack. It's Michael."

"Hey, Mikey, my man. How is it?"

Jack spoke as cleverly as he had answered the phone. Though to most people, Jack would appear to be the exact opposite of the kind of friend from high school that you would stay in touch with. Yet, for Michael, Jack was the perfect candidate. He was overall a nice enough guy, but he was still just out on the rim of reality enough that, when Michael stayed with Jack, he could come and go freely and not be too involved in the actual "visiting" that would be required with an old friend. Jack was as low maintenance as any human being could ever be.

"Hey, I'm coming into town in a few hours. Just wanted to let you know, and to see if it was cool if I stayed with you?"

Michael was highly conscious of the way he chose his words when speaking with Jack, especially on the phone. He knew it was rather juvenile, but it was the natural response when speaking to someone using this kind of language to simply repeat.

"Sure thing, man. Door's open."

The last two words of the conversation were the two reasons that Jack was the perfect friend.

The drive always went by much faster than any one person would assume a three-hour drive would go. With the moon rising high, Michael pulled into town around midnight.

It was quaint. At least, that's how it's residents referred to it. The church steeple stood high above all else in the center of town. The elementary school sat directly underneath it. Just down the street, a small post office and hardware store were neighbors. The tiny houses fanned out in all directions from that point with small businesses and shops peppered throughout. Most of those houses were equipped with porches, as the local habit was spending evenings sitting on the front porch and striking up conversations with neighbors and passers-by.

His mother's house sat just along the main road that weaved through the town. He drove past on his way to Jack's place. All the lights were out, and the garage door was pulled shut.

Jack's place wasn't much to look at, but at the same time, it was nice for a "pushing thirty bachelor pad". It was a single story brick house. Small rectangular windows lined the foundation of the house, and the light poured out through them, Jack was in the basement as usual. He would leave the back door unlocked, always, unafraid of intruders due to his ravenous beagle running about the chain link fence that outlined his back yard. The dog was actually none of the sort, as it licked furiously at Michael's hand as he opened the gate to get to the back door.

Once inside, Michael walked to the back of the house where the guest room was waiting for him. He set his bag down on the bed and kicked off his shoes. Tired from the road trip, he rubbed at his eyes as he walked down to say hello to Jack.

"Jack, hey Jack?" he called out.

"Hey, Michael! You made it okay!"

Jack got up from his beanbag chair and turned down the volume on the television where some random 80's hair band was dancing about and shredding guitars. He walked over to Michael and extended his arms for a hug.

"Good to see you, brother," Jack exclaimed.

"Gotta be honest, man, long drive," Michael said, indicating a quick retreat to the guest room for a good night's sleep.

"Sure man, you know where it is." As Michael began back up the stairs, Jack called out to him: "Good to see you, man."

Michael stopped and peeked back around the corner as Jack spoke again.

"And, I'm really sorry about your mom, man."

"Thanks, Jack."

Part Nine

There was a loud banging at the front door of Jack's place. Michael knew two things: first that Jack would not be getting up to answer it, and second, that it was his sister, Lily. Lily lived in an apartment just up the street from his mother's house. She was an avid jogger, rarely missing a morning run before school. Jack's house was right on her jogging route, and as the early morning light peeked through the drawn shades, he knew it was her.

Out back, the vicious attack dog was pacing the fence and barking. A few more knocks and he drug himself from bed. He answered the door, expecting a wagging finger being thrown in his face.

She burst in and threw her arms around him. "Michael!" she exclaimed.

Taken aback by the affection, Michael wrapped his arms around her. She was very petite, and much shorter than him. Her blonde hair poked out from underneath an old baseball cap. She squeezed him tight.

"I can't believe you're here! I'm so glad you're here," she spoke so enthusiastically.

"Yeah, I came," he said.

She stepped back from him to take a good hard look at her brother. "Well, you've been writing, huh?"

He knew she was commenting on the rough appearance; the shaggy hair and beard. He nervously scratched away at his cheeks as she observed him so closely.

A deep breath and a smile as she spoke again: "I'm so glad you are here."

"Well, yeah, I mean..." he paused, "how could I not come?"

"I've been thinking about you so much lately."

Michael's head still spun, his sister's reaction to seeing him the complete opposite of what he had expected. She seemed so genuinely happy to see him. For a moment, he felt such guilt for having not answered her phone calls the last time she was in the city.

"Mom keeps asking about you. She never says more than that, but it's every other time I see her. And I see her everyday now."

"Well, that's good I guess. I..." he paused again, not wanting to spoil the warm feeling he had from his sister's company, "figured you would be angry with me."

"Angry? No, Michael." She shook her head as the thought went back through her mind. "No."

"Well, I know the others are..."

"The others, yes. I'm not going to lie to you, the others are pretty mad. George is probably the worst. He actually says it out loud sometimes."

Michael's face turned stern, the apparent truth being confirmed.

"You have to understand, Michael," she spoke as she reached out and grabbed his hand. "The five of us here never changed. We are all still really close and we all struggle to understand where you are coming from. We don't really get it, and to be fair, you don't really help us get it."

"I know, Lily," he said, searching for the words to describe his complete and utter escape from the kind of closeness his siblings had. "It's just that, I have to be alone to really work, and it's not a personal thing at all. It's just who I am. I know that's hard to understand, being the only one of six that isn't like the rest."

"Well, you could just say that. In fact, that's more than I've heard you speak in a long time. Even at Christmas, you were so withdrawn. I just..." she sighed before speaking again, "I miss you."

With that said, she threw her arms around him again.

"So, are you going to see mom today?"

"Yeah, that's the plan. Do you know what her schedule is like today?"

"I'm pretty sure George is taking her to a doctor's appointment this morning, but the afternoon should be good. She hasn't been feeling too well lately, so she doesn't do a whole lot."

"Okay, thanks Lil'," he smiled, having called her by her childhood nickname.

"How long will you be around?" she asked.

"I figured a day or two for sure, spend some time with mom and see how she is doing."

"Okay. Well I should get going. Maybe dinner or something?" She smiled as she turned away and resumed her jog down the street.

Still completely overwhelmed by the warm reception from his baby sister, Michael sat at Jack's kitchen table. Jack had already come through on his way to work. Cup of coffee in front of him, Michael's mind quickly went to George. He was dreading arriving at his mother's house, and the chance that George would still be there. He knew it was unavoidable, at some point he would have to face George again; and for that matter, the others too.

He had gotten the typewriter out and set it up on the table in front of him, hoping for the off chance that he might get a few pages churned out before he headed over to see his mother. But he had too much on his mind to focus for more than a few moments. He kept finding himself standing in the backyard smoking, as Jack didn't allow smoking in his house (at least not cigarettes). The beagle playfully pawed at his feet, egging on another toss of his tennis ball. Michael complied, and the pup bounded off after it, his short legs tangling beneath him.

It was unseasonably cool for an August day, a slight breeze coming across the yard. Though only less than two hundred miles north of the city, Michael was amazed at how much difference there actually was between the city and out here in the country.

Michael peeked in through the window to check the time on the clock that hung above the kitchen sink. He was just killing time until he could go see his mother.

Already a chain smoker in the most deliberate sense of the word, Michael's nerves kept an even more constant stream of cigarettes parked between his narrow lips. Again the dog came back, dropping the ball and pawing away at his jeans. As he bent to throw the ball, he knew the dog would demand this for hours on end if he'd allow it. Luckily, he was only a half of an hour from heading over to his mother's house.

His heart sank as he saw the black sedan in the driveway as he pulled up to his mother's house. Though he hadn't seen the car before, he assumed it belonged to George. He pulled in next to it, and slowly got out of his car. He was in no hurry to head inside and face the music.

His mother's house was big, far too big for a widowed mother of adults living alone. It was where he grew up and his parents raised their family. The front door opened into the dining room and kitchen. When Michael walked in, George stood at the kitchen counter, and he appeared to be making a sandwich.

"Uh… hello, George," he spoke nervously.

George froze. Setting down the knife he was holding, he turned to Michael.

"Michael. I didn't know you were in town."

"Yeah, I drove down last night. Stayed with Jack. I came to see mom."

He expected the worst from his brother. George's face was as hard and stern as his father's had been. Michael tried to read his brother: his reaction, his mood, any kind of indication that would help guide Michael to say the right things.

"Well, I am glad you did. She just laid down for a quick nap."

George was short with his words. Michael spoke to break the tension.

"Listen, about the last time you saw me, I..."

"Nope," was all he said. He put a hand up and shook his head. "It doesn't matter. The important thing is that you came. But, you do not get to come in here and make excuses for yourself."

"George, I am not trying to make excuses. You caught me on a bad night, and..."

Again he was cut off. The hand now pushed out farther, motioning for him to hold his tongue.

"I really have no desire to hear about your bad nights, or even your good nights. Now," he slowly lowered his hand, "Like I said, it's good that you are here."

"George, if you would just let me explain," Michael pleaded.

"Stop! Michael, stop! You don't deserve that. You cut us out! You walked away from us." His eyes got wide, and a primal gaze came over them. "Dad died and instead of leaning on us or being there for us, you left. You walked away, Michael! You understand that, don't you! You understand that we were all left here, wondering why. Why would you just turn your back on us?"

He grew more and more animated as his speech went on.

"And it's sad, Michael. It's sad to me to think that it took your mother getting sick to bring you back home! Don't you think that's sad?"

Michael stood there and took it, realizing how long this must have been building inside him. He was, in all cases now, the man of the family. His whole life, George had taken his siblings troubles on his own shoulders, always willing to help, always willing to sacrifice, and when he couldn't help, always willing to sympathize and listen. He felt the anger and hurt in his words, and he knew that it was not just George he was hearing from. George spoke for them all.

"But, yes, Michael it is good that you are here. But don't you think for a second that we just forget the past few years; that we forget that we don't even know you anymore!"

George began pointing at Michael, pumping his hand forward every time he spoke the word 'you'.

"You are a stranger to me. Your mother wants you here, but as far as I am concerned, I couldn't give a damn!"

George's rant broke only when from the bedroom just off of the kitchen, their mother walked into the room. She looked at George, all red and finger waving. Then, she looked to Michael and her face lit up.

"Michael!" she spoke. A wide smile came across her face as she rushed across the room to greet her son.

Michael had thought an awful lot about his mother since the meeting with George and hearing of her illness. He knew that it would be difficult seeing her, but he was not prepared for the intense wave of emotion that came over him as she walked toward him with her arms outstretched.

She was weeping by the time she got to him, and she wrapped her arms around him and squeezed him. He did the same. The embrace lasted more than a minute.

"Please, come in and sit with me, Michael," she said as she led him to the kitchen table.

As the two sat down, George spoke up: "Your sandwich is ready for you here whenever you get hungry okay?"

"Oh, George, I told you you didn't need to make it for me. But, thank you, son."

"I'm going to get going then. I'll stop back by later on to see you, okay."

He walked over to her and kissed her on the cheek. All he threw at Michael as he passed was a cold glare.

"Bye, Michael."

"Bye, George."

As George pulled the door closed behind him, Michael's attention turned back to his mother. He could see how much the years had taken their toll on her. She was pushing sixty now, and her eyes were heavy. Her brown hair was graying and thin. She wore small oval glasses.

"Tell me, Michael, how have you been?" She looked at him hard, as if she was relearning his face.

"Well, um," he spoke nervously, as if his explanation needed to warrant his absence. "I've been okay."

She reached across the table and placed her hand on his. "Michael, tell me."

He sighed, and realized she wasn't looking for theatrics. She just wanted to hear the truth.

"I have been struggling, mom. It hasn't been good for a while now. But, there is hope. My editor just pitched a novel I'm working on, and it might do something."

"Well, that's great news, Michael. How wonderful." She looked at his face, and the lack of excitement he showed while speaking of the novel. "Tell me more about the first part."

"I was, uh, am lost, mom. I went the last few years trying so hard to write another one. With everything I had, I just wanted to get back to that place where I was confident in what I was doing."

She repositioned herself at the table, and leaned in to listen better.

"The first book validated me. But, then, as time passed it didn't matter anymore, because I wasn't writing anything good. It was all just awful. I put so much pressure on myself all the time..."

He found himself just hemorrhaging all the feelings that he had kept bottled for so long. His mother sat there listening, not judging, but listening.

"I understand, Michael. You are so much like your father in that way, ya know. There was never a limit to how far he would push himself."

She smiled when she spoke of him, but for Michael it was much different. Just at the mention of him, his eyes welled immediately. He turned his head away, not wanting his mother to see how much it affected him.

"You miss him, don't you, Michael," she whispered, gripping his hand in hers. He was crying now. "Me, too."

There was a pause as Michael attempted to compose himself.

"Come now, this is a happy occasion. Let's leave that for another time. Tell me about this new story, then?"

He wiped his face as he turned back to his mother. She always did love his stories.

"Well, to be honest, the story is based around a woman struggling to find herself. Kind of a quarter life crisis thing." He looked to his mother, almost shyly. "The heroine is based a lot on Amy."

"Oh, Amy?" She sat back in her chair as Michael watched her closely to gauge her reaction. "Do you stay in touch with Amy at all?"

"No. I haven't spoken to her in a long time."

"Do you still think about Amy, Michael?"

"Yeah, I do, mom. I do think about her a lot. And, I'm not sure why. I mean, when we were together, I was so focused on writing that I didn't think enough of her to make her stay with me. Now, it's been a few years and I think about her all the time."

"Well, Michael, thinking of someone means a lot of different things. Maybe you are just lonely, and thinking of her Amy makes you feel like you weren't always alone, and maybe you won't be lonely forever. Like remembering your relationship with her is a way of keeping hope for the future."

"Or, maybe you just miss the friend you had before the two of you got together. The split between you two wasn't very good, and so you completely lost her. Remember how close you guys were in high school? That was years before you ever got together."

"Then there's always the chance that you still love her."

She squeezed his hand. Michael found himself very

emotional sitting with his mother, much more than he ever allowed himself to be when alone.

"She called me a few days ago."

Michael perked up. "Oh, really?"

"Yeah, her folks had told her about me being sick. She was calling to see how I was feeling. We chatted for a bit."

"That's really nice of her. How is she?" He eagerly awaited the answer. Just hearing his mother mention her name got his heart racing.

"She's good. She's living in St. Louis now, working at a law firm. Just a secretary, but she said it's a great job and she's close to her sister who just had a baby, so…"

Michael took a minute to take in what his mother said. He could see Amy there, sitting behind a desk in some uptight lawyer's office, probably hating it but saying things like 'it's a good job'. She was an eternal optimist. That's why she stayed with him as long as she did. She would say 'he's such a good guy, he's just really focused.' He could see her holding her sister's baby; she loved kids so much. She was good at the baby voices.

He smiled.

"Michael?" his mother questioned.

"It's very strange, mom. I spend so much time in my own head, and so many hours working so hard, sometimes I forget people move on. People are living their lives."

"Yeah, well, everyone does that in their own way, Michael. I'm sure that you aren't the same man I used to know either. But, at your core, you are still that kid sitting at the kitchen table scribbling in notebooks all hours of the night."

"I just feel like I've missed so much; and by choice. I chose to hide away and make up my own stories. Now, I've screwed up so much."

"People make choices, Michael. But, not everything is lost."

"George is so angry with me."

"Sure, George is angry, now. Maybe they're all angry now. But that doesn't mean that they'll be angry forever. The important thing is that you determine what you do. If you don't come around by choice, I can handle that. That means to me, that you are choosing to live your life the way you want to live it. If you start coming around because you feel like you 'owe' it to someone, then you are allowing other people to determine your life."

His mother's words were hitting him hard; advice he needed to hear.

"George is angry. But, he's angry about a lot of things. He doesn't like the fact that Vicky divorced him. He doesn't like his job. Now, why is that, do you think? George always considered other people when he made his choices. When George got out of high school, he wanted to make a lot of money and prove himself to your father. So, when he went off to college, he studied business and marketing. When he was choosing jobs, he was about to get married. He took the highest offer. Now, he's divorced and he goes to that job everyday because he doesn't know any different."

She leaned back in and stared Michael in the eye.

"You, son, you live your life the way you want to. You write stories because it's what you are passionate about. No one can ever take that from you, or tell you stop doing it. But, we are family. And no matter how long it takes, or how many years you need to be off doing your own thing, family never completely goes away."

"Your brother is angry, but he won't be forever. When you are ready, if you are ever ready, they will be waiting for you, Michael."

His mother spoke of time as if it was guaranteed. Suddenly, he realized the weight of what she was saying.

"I guess what I really mean is, I..." as he spoke he began choking up. "I just, I'm so sorry I missed all this time I could have spent with you."

He cried openly in front his mother now. He was ashamed

of neglecting her for years, and now she could be gone so soon.

"Michael, I may be sick, but it's not going to kill me tomorrow. The doctors say that they caught it very early on, and that a few rounds of chemo may completely beat it."

She began rubbing his back as he hung his head.

"It's just a really scary word. No one wants to hear it, because it carries such a heavy tone. But, Michael, I am going to fight this thing with all that I have."

She sat back in her seat and looked up. "I miss your father so much, but I am not ready to see him again. Not yet."

She waited a minute before she spoke again, standing from the table as she did so.

"Now, enough with all this, do you want some cookies?"

She walked to the refrigerator and pulled out a jug of milk. Her cookies were legendary, and Michael smiled at her quick split from the heavy conversation they were having.

She brought a plate with a few cookies on it to the table and two glasses of milk.

"So, really, mom, how are you feeling?"

"Most of the time, I'm fine. The doctors have put me on some medication for a week before we start the first round of chemotherapy. Usually after I take it, I feel kind of sick for while. But, the rest of the time, I'm fine."

She turned the conversation back to Michael.

"So, how long do you think you are gonna stay?"

"Well, a couple days at most, for now at least. My editor is going to kill me for leaving the city, I'm kind of on a deadline."

"So, this one is really going somewhere, huh?" she questioned.

"Yeah, the publishers are on board. I just have to finish it. I've been blocked for a few days. It's frustrating."

"Well, I can understand that. I was really upset with

George for driving down to talk to you. I mean, I'm glad he was concerned, but I knew that was going to get you down."

"Well, if I called more often, or at all, he wouldn't have had to drive down and tell me. This whole thing has been such a..."

"Kick in the pants," she said with a smile. He smiled back at her.

She spoke again: "Sometimes, you just need a little jolt. That's how I feel, at least. Makes you take stock of things."

There was another short pause, and then she spoke again.

"Well, I know Millie and Sam are both out of town. Millie is in Vegas at a convention, and Sam's either in Chicago or Milwaukee, that sales job keeps him moving so much, ya know. But, I'm sure the others would love to see you. I don't mean to rush you off, but I need to go lie down for a while. The doctors upped my dosage at my appointment today."

"Okay, mom," he said as he stood and hugged her.

"Michael, just be patient with them. They are more hurt then angry, but it's family. They'll come around."

He turned to head for the door, and she called out to him: "And Michael, make sure you stop by before you head back out of town. I have something to give you before you leave. Okay?"

"Okay, mom. Will do. Sleep well."

He turned and headed out the door. As he made his way to his car, he reflected on the conversation and what his mother had said. He had worried so much about the reaction she would have to him, but she spoke to him like she understood exactly where he was coming from.

It was a mixture of guilt and happiness. The wind was blowing and the children were running out of the school a block away. People waved as they drove past. Michael was happy to be home.

Part Ten

The phone in shirt pocket began ringing just as he was pulling back into Jack's driveway. He was lost in a daydream and tapping the steering wheel in time with the music coming from the radio. The second ring snapped him back to reality.

"Hello?" he answered.

"Michael, it's Frank."

Michael froze, quickly turning the killing the radio and switching the car off. He knew this call was coming.

"Frank, hello. How are you?" Michael asked.

"I could be better Michael. I could be better." There was a pause before he spoke again. "How are we doing on those pages? Any progress?"

"Well, to be honest, Frank," Michael braced himself before he continued, "there has been no progress. I had some personal things that I had to attend to. I am actually out of the city for a few days."

There was a long pause. Michael cringed, pulling the phone away from his ear as he waited for Frank's reaction.

"Well, that explains why you weren't answering your home phone."

'That was it?' Michael thought. 'No way that's it.' He couldn't believe that was the extent of his reaction.

"I have to be honest with you, Michael," Frank spoke again. "I'm a bit disappointed. Do you know what it took for me to get the pitch for this book?"

"I both understand and appreciate what you have done for me, Frank. I mean, this whole time. You are such a big part of my success. I just had some things that I needed to take care of here."

"Well, I guess I'm a bit relieved, to be completely honest."

"Oh," Michael reacted, trying to understand what Frank

meant.

"Ever since your first book deal, all I have known you to do is sit in that apartment and write. Now, there's nothing wrong with that, but I must say that I'm glad to hear that you have other things to care about."

Michael laughed a bit to himself. Here was Frank, a hard-nosed bottom line businessman, and he was worried Michael was insane.

"What I am saying is, how long are you going to be away and when can I realistically expect those pages?"

"I'm heading back tomorrow. I'll get right back to work on it." Michael sighed, thinking of the talk he had just had with his mother. He felt much more confident than when he left the city. "I will check in with you at the end of the week. As soon as I can get you the pages, I will."

"Okay," Frank began. "I'll let the publishers know that they'll just have to wait a few more days for it. I'm sure it'll be worth it."

Michael smiled. He had dreaded this phone call since the moment he started driving from the city. He was a bit shocked to say the least.

"Thanks, Frank. I know that you worked really hard to get me the pitch. I am sorry that I can't get you the pages sooner like I said I could."

"Michael, listen. A few days is no big deal. The bottom line is, I need those pages. I make the deals, it's what I do. I don't write the books. You have things that need to be done, that's fine. Just keep me in the loop here. I may make my money off of you, but that doesn't mean that's all I'm worried about."

Needless to say, Michael was relieved. As he hung up the phone, he got out of his car. He tossed away his cigarette as he made his way around the back of the house. He opened the gate as the dog bounced behind it, tennis ball in mouth and waiting for him. He gave the ball a toss across the yard, giving himself just enough time to make it to the back door before the dog could chase it down and come back for another toss.

As he passed the kitchen table, he saw a note that Jack had left for him.

"Hey Mikey, when I was home for lunch, Lily called and invited you to dinner at her and Nate's place. 7 o'clock."

Michael smiled as read it. Setting the note down, he made his way back to the guest room. He picked his bag up from the floor tossing it onto the bed. He quickly pulled some clothes out and laid them out on the bed.

He then made his way back to the kitchen and took a seat behind his typewriter. He smiled to himself as he loaded a fresh piece of paper. He glanced over the last few pages from the folder he set next to the typewriter.

He took a deep breath and began typing away. He worked busily, and without his signature coffee and cigarettes, continuously wrote for the next few hours.

The steam from the shower had the mirror fogged up. He worked at getting his pants on, followed by his shirt. Quickly wiping the fog away with his hand, he pulled a comb through his hair. He laughed as looked at the remaining crack in his lower lip. It had healed nicely over the course of a few days. He scratched away at his beard as he brushed his teeth.

He walked down the hall into the kitchen to check the time. Jack stood there, eating a slice of pizza over a napkin.

"Jack, when did you get in?" he asked.

"Just a few minutes ago. Brought a pizza if you're hungry man." He was still wearing his uniform from work, light blue button down shirt and dark blue Dickies. His pants were covered in mud.

"Long day there," Michael asked, pointing to the stains.

"Yeah, new house just out of town. The plumbers busted a pipe just outside the crawl space entrance yesterday. Guess where

I had to work all day? In and out all day long." He pushed the last bit of pizza crust left in his hand into his mouth, then threw his hands up in the air. "The show must go on."

Michael laughed, the pizza nearly falling out of his mouth as Jack played air guitar and jumped around the kitchen. He was always reenacting the rock shows of his glory days.

"I take it you saw the note I left for you?" Jack asked, shoving another mouthful into his mouth.

"Yeah man, thanks. I'm heading over there in a few. Gotta finish getting ready."

"Cool beans. Tell Lily and Nate I said hey."

Making his way back to the bathroom, he tucked his shirt in. One more quick look in the mirror and he was out the door.

There was a hardware store in the center of town that sat across from the post office. It was a two-story building. Back when the store first opened, the man that owned the store lived on the second floor. His whole life he lived up there. When he passed and the store was handed down to his sons, they began renting the second floor out. Once Lily got back to town from college, she began living there. It was small, and out of date, but it was relatively cheap; perfect for a single teacher just starting out.

Michael didn't know Nate all that well. He was a teacher as well. He taught history at the high school. Michael met him the few times that he visited over the past few years. Nate seemed like a good enough guy. He fit perfectly into the tall, dark, and handsome category.

The steps leading up to the second story apartment were old and rickety, creaking loudly with each step Michael took. 'Perhaps an early security alarm system' Michael thought to himself and laughed. He puffed quickly at his cigarette, trying to finish it before reaching the door. Lily despised cigarettes.

She answered the door with a smile. Her blonde hair was all done up and she wore a jeans and a bright pink cardigan.

"Michael, you got the message!" She threw her arms

around him and gave him a big hug.

"Yeah, Jack left it for me. So, here I am."

"Ugh," she exclaimed as she pulled away from him. "You smell like death!"

She was mocking him, smelling the cigarettes on him. He laughed as he followed her into the apartment.

The small living room wore a couch, a chair and the TV. Michael chuckled to himself when he saw the awful green shag carpeting under his feet.

"Where's Nate?" he asked, having expected to see him sitting on the couch.

"He got called away. There was a big fire out on Johnson road somewhere. Hay barn or something," she answered.

"Oh, he volunteers?"

"Yeah. Just started last year. A couple of the guys on his softball team were firefighters and they kind of recruited him I guess." She made her way into the kitchen and opened the stove, checking whatever was cooking. "He'll probably be stuck out there all night. Those barn fires take forever."

"Oh, well, that's unfortunate. I was looking forward to getting to talk with him."

Lily smiled at him. A rare thing to hear her brother say, she shook her head.

Michael made his way to the couch and sat down.

"Do you want something to drink, Michael?" she called out from the kitchen.

"Yeah, that would be great. Do you need any help in there?" He stood and turned to the kitchen.

Lily walked out of the kitchen, handed him a beer, and said: "No, no. You just sit and relax."

She quickly headed back into the kitchen.

"So, you saw mom today?" she asked.

"Yeah. I did." Michael smiled to himself. "It was really great. I am so glad that I came."

"That's great, Michael. I am glad you came too. Was George still there, then?" she asked.

Michael laughed out loud. "Huh, yes he was. Boy, did he lay into me, too."

Lily walked back into the living room and sat in the chair across from him.

"He is so angry with me. The minute I walked in, he just let me hear it."

"Well, that's George. He's always held grudges, Michael." She laughed. "Do you remember when George was in high school, and his girlfriend dumped him?"

"Yeah. That was a bad year."

"Yeah. Three months later, three months!, she starts dating his buddy Alan."

"And George socked him in second period math. I remember, he got suspended for three days for that!"

They laughed.

"George hasn't gone to a single high school reunion because of Alan. He hasn't spoken to him since!"

"Wow. I didn't know that."

"Listen, George is amazing. But, just like everyone else, for every good thing about George, there's a bad thing right behind it. You might not see them all the time, but they are there. I mean," she giggled again. "You have probably seen more of them than me."

They laughed again. Michael stared at his sister. He couldn't help but have this huge knot of guilt in his stomach, having missed conversations like this for so long.

"Did you know Rose is coming, too?"

Michael perked up. "Really? I did not know that."

"Yeah, I called her today and told you were in town. She said she would come and see you."

"Wow. That's great news. I figured she would be more on the George side than anything."

"Well, we all miss you Michael. Some people show it differently. All she said was that she would come, nothing else. Take it as a positive, I guess."

Michael sipped at his beer as Lily went back to busying herself in the kitchen. It wasn't long until there was a knock on the door. Michael stood and went to the door to open it.

"Rose?" he answered as he opened the door.

She resembled his mother much more than Lily did. She was a short woman, her brown hair starting to gray like his mother's did. She wore thick-rimmed glasses.

"Michael," was all she said as she came in and gave him a big hug.

The two walked into the apartment as Lily came from the kitchen to greet her sister.

"Rose, hey, how was work?" she asked as the two hugged.

"Not too bad at all, Lily. I take it Nate's not here, I saw the fire out on Johnson road on my way. I could see the flames from the interstate."

"Yeah, he got called out a few hours ago. How about a beer?"

"Sounds good, thanks." Rose made her way to the couch and sat down next to Michael.

"So, Michael. It's been a while. How have you been?" she asked. She was more an intimidating presence than Lily. Michael could not quite decipher whether she was angry with him.

"Well, I've just been writing and getting by." He was nervous, and quickly turned the focus onto her. "How is the hospital?"

"I'm not there anymore. Nope, took a job with Dr. Richards.

He started a private practice and took me along with him."

"Oh, well, that's great for you. Do you like that better than the hospital?"

"Definitely. I'm the head nurse in his office. Plus, he's a great doctor to work for."

"And how long ago was this?"

"It was last year, August actually."

There was an awkward silence. Her tone began to grow more serious. Michael had even been home for Christmas last year, and didn't know this.

His palms were sweating. He rubbed them on the legs of his pants. Lily came to his rescue.

"Rose, did you get that new car you were talking about a few weeks ago?"

"No, not yet. The deals will be better at the end of the year. Then, I might trade up."

Lily looked for a way to keep the conversation going, sensing her brother's anxiety.

"Hey, Michael and I were just talking about that time in high school when George got suspended for hitting Alan Holmes?"

Rose laughed wryly. "Yes, I do. George cold-cocked him. He deserved it too, he stole George's girlfriend."

"No he did not," Lily laughed out. "She dumped George months before that ever happened! What are you talking about?" She was egging Rose on playfully.

"Are you kidding me, Lily? She didn't dump George until that Alan kid was after her."

Lily laughed out again. "You are dreaming, Rose. We all know that George was just holding that grudge like he always does!"

Rose started laughing as well. Old family stories always had them locked into playful arguments.

"What do you think, Michael?" Rose asked. "Do you remember?"

Michael smiled nervously. "All I remember is that for three weeks after that, they were too busy yelling at George to yell at me!"

The three laughed.

"Yeah, dad was always on your case," Lily said.

"Oh, come on, don't be so naïve. He had it coming!" Rose exclaimed. "Michael was always causing trouble. Do you remember when we were little and a GI Joe SWAT team came busting into my Barbie dream house and destroyed it!"

"That wasn't me, that was Sam," Michael retorted.

"But, where did little Sammy get the idea, Michael? From one of your stories that you had just read to him!"

"Well, don't worry too much about that, Michael. Because she pretty much just came in and took my Barbie dream house into her room!"

"I don't know to what you are referencing, Lily!" Rose blurted.

The tension was officially broken as the three laughed uncontrollably.

They traded war stories from their childhood back and forth as Lily finished cooking. They sat down at the table, continuing the reminiscing.

After a while, they all had finished their meal. They sat around the small table in kitchen, dirty plates and wine glasses sitting in front of them.

A quiet moment came. The three looked at each other.

Rose was the first to speak. "It really is good that you came, Michael."

"I'm sorry that it took so long, Rose. I really am."

"Well, I'm really glad you are here," Lily added.

"I just don't really get it, I guess is the problem. I don't understand how you just move away and that's it. I mean, we see you at Christmas, and you say nothing. I don't think we said hardly anything to each other that day."

Rose stared at him now. She wasn't angry, it was hurt that Michael saw in her eyes.

"It's hard to explain, Rose."

Rose turned her eyes down to her wine glass as she pulled it up for a drink.

"I see now, how it looks. I didn't before. It looks like I don't give a damn about you guys. I get that. When I put out my first book, it was the first time since dad died and Amy left me that I had anything to be proud of. I moved away and I locked myself in a room day and night, trying to get that back. As time passed, the writing kept getting worse, and I got farther and farther from it. I also got farther and farther from you all. Before I knew, I was so convinced that you all had written me off that I just stayed away, avoided you all. I was so lost, and I thought that no one would really understand."

Rose studied his face, seeing the pain in his eyes as he spoke.

"Haven't we always been there, though? The whole time growing up, we were all there for each other. Why would you just shut us out?"

"I don't really know how to explain it any better. When dad died," Michael's eyes began welling up, "I didn't know how to handle it. Nothing really made sense anymore. The only thing I could do to cope was write. That's why I lost Amy, all I did was write and drink and smoke and then write some more."

Lily sat across the table watching her brother try to explain himself. Rose was stone faced, trying to understand what Michael was saying. She couldn't really though, and Lily saw it. But, there was nothing that Lily could say to help.

"It's selfish."

Michael looked at her. Two simple words she spoke. But, they were true; perfectly true. He searched for something more that he could say.

"So, have you gotten to see mom?" Rose asked, breaking the awkward silence.

Michael snapped back to reality, grateful for the turn in conversation.

"Yeah, I saw her today. She looks pretty good, considering."

"She has stayed spunky. That medicine they put her on keeps her feeling bad, but she is always positive when I see her," Lily spoke up.

"Yeah, it's only the beginning, unfortunately, for that. The chemo is going to be tough." Rose spoke. "She's really lucky that they caught it early enough."

"Do you think that they will get it with just chemo, Rose?" Michael asked.

"Honestly, it's a roll of the dice. I mean, it's pretty likely that it won't take more than a few rounds to actually kill all the cells. The kicker is the recurrence."

"What do you mean?" Michael asked again.

"More often than not, the cells can come back. If we can get her healthy this time, we really have to be careful of that. Lots of doctor visits."

"Whatever it takes," Lily added. "I'm just glad they found it now."

"We're lucky," Rose said. "Not too many people get this lucky."

There was a long pause. The three of them all let the thought sink in.

"I really should get going," Rose said as she stood from the table. "Do you want some help cleaning up, Lil?"

"No, no. I know you have an early shift in the morning." Lily started gathering the plates from table. "I'll take care of it. Am

I going to see you on Saturday?"

"Yes, I will be there. The party starts at 3, right?" Rose asked.

"Yeah. Here at 3."

"Alright, then I'll see you." The two hugged and Rose started to head for the door.

Michael followed her out. "It was really good to see you, Rose."

She turned and looked to him. He could still see confusion in her eyes.

"You too, Michael."

She opened her arms for a hug. He wrapped his arms around her.

"And don't be such a stranger, okay?" she whispered.

As she made her way out the door, Rose called back to him: "And steer clear of George. He's really mad at you." She laughed as she closed the door behind her.

Michael smiled and called out: "Will do."

He made his way back into the kitchen to help Lily.

"Dinner was great, Lil. Thank you."

She smiled at him as she dropped the plates into the sink. "Anytime, Michael."

"And thanks for inviting Rose. I know she's still upset, but I felt like…"

He was interrupted. "She'll come around. They all will." She smiled.

"I hope so."

Lily busied herself back and forth from the table.

"Here, let me help you." He brought the wine glasses to the counter.

Lily started some dishwater in the sink and began washing the plates. Michael grabbed a towel and started to dry them as she handed them to him.

"Is it true? What you were saying about dad?" she asked.

"What do you mean?"

"That you are still dealing with him dying, and that's why you left?"

"Well," he looked to her, her eyes heavy and sad. "Mostly, yeah. I just keep seeing that day, that party they had for me when I got back from New York, remember that writing contest. The look he had all day, I see it all the time."

Lily smiled and spoke: "He was so proud of you. The whole time you were in New York, he would brag to the neighbors, the grocery check out girl, any and everyone."

"When my first book got published, all I could think about was: "What would he have said? How would he have reacted?" All I ever wanted was for him to still be here for it."

They both were getting choked up. Michael wiped a tear from his eye.

Lily spoke again: "I know. There was this time I was in the play at school. I had maybe three lines, but he was right there in the front row watching me so closely. I always remember that when I think of him."

"George and Sam had baseball. He always went to games and he was always so proud of his boys. All I had was writing, and..." he stopped.

"I know, Michael," Lily said, putting her hand on his. "We all miss him."

"And now, with mom, I just..." he struggled to finish his sentence.

"She's going to be fine. You heard Rose. She sees this all the time. She's going to be fine!"

"Thanks, Lily. It took a lot for me to come, and you are making it so much easier." He gave his sister a big hug.

The two stepped back and went back to washing the dishes.

They both composed themselves.

Then, Lily spoke again: "So, is this new project any good?"

"Frank, my editor, has already pitched it to the publisher and they want to publish it."

"Oh my God, Michael. That's great news!" She put her hand up, looking for a high five.

Michael laughed as she waited, and then complied.

"Is it finished yet?" she asked.

"No," he said. "I am almost done. But, with the mom thing, I have been pretty scatterbrained lately."

"You still using that typewriter dad got you?"

"Yeah, it's at Jack's place now," Michael laughed.

"Well then, what are you doing here? Get over there and write!"

She dried her hands and began pushing him toward the door.

He laughed. She continued to push him, though.

"I mean it, you go. I need you to finish that book!"

He put his shoes on, and stood at the door.

"Okay, okay. Thanks, Lil," he said as he hugged her again.

"I'll be at school until 3 if you want to stop by and say hey before you hit the road back home, okay?"

"Will do," he said as he turned and opened the door.

As he made his way down the stairs, his sister stood watching him leave.

She called out to him: "I love you, Michael. Always have, always will."

He smiled.

Part Eleven

The cool breeze was still hanging around as Michael drove back to Jack's place. Windows down and the radio loud, he flicked a cigarette out the window. It wasn't too late, and many of the houses along the way still had occupants on the front porches. They all waved as he passed. They didn't know him, it was just what they did when a car drove through their sleepy little town. Michael smiled and waved back.

It wasn't far to Jack's, but he tried to squeeze another cigarette in. He pulled into Jack's driveway and shut the car off. The Townes Van Zandt classic "If I Needed You" was on the radio, so he sat and listened until it was over. He smiled every time Emmylou started singing her parts. He loved this song.

When it finished, he stepped out of the car. He began walking around to the back of the house. Again, the dog was waiting, tennis ball in mouth. Michael laughed as he latched the gate behind him. The dog dropped the ball at his feet, and began licking away at his hand, undiscouraged by the cigarette perched in between his fingers.

"Alright, alright," he said as he bent to grab the ball. He flung it across the yard. It was dark, and he could hear the dog fumbling through the weeds that lined the fence. As Michael puffed again on his cigarette, the dog came back into site, as if to check to make sure he had actually thrown it.

Again the dog ran back into the dark corner of the yard. Michael laughed a bit, as he finished the cigarette. He headed inside, the dog still foraging against the fence.

The house was dark except for the light coming from the stairway leading down to the basement where Michael was sure Jack sat worshiping the gods of rock.

He sat down at the table behind the typewriter. A quick roll of the head and crack of the fingers, and he was off, typing away.

After a while, Jack came up from the basement. He walked past Michael en route to the refrigerator. He pulled a pizza box out and set it down on the stove.

"Got some pizza left over, Mikey," he began, shoving a piece in his mouth, "if you want some."

"Thanks, Jack. I appreciate it, man."

"How did dinner with the family go, then?"

"It was really good. I got to see two of my sisters. We hung out for a while, just caught up."

"They still pissed?" Jack asked, knowing that tensions between Michael and the family was the exact reason Michael stayed with him when he was in town.

"Coming around, I guess. Hard to say just yet."

"Glad to hear it, Mikey. You heading out tomorrow?"

"Yeah, probably afternoonish."

"Cool man, well, I'll be working so, I guess we'll see ya the next go round, eh?"

"Yeah man, thanks for letting me crash. You're a good dude, Jack."

Jack began back down the stairs, but paused just long enough to holler back up at Michael. "Dude, I found this old E.L.O concert some dude bootlegged in Toronto. E.L.O. man! Come down and check it out, if you want."

He kept on down the stairs as Michael laughed to himself. He could hear Jack plop back down in the beanbag chair followed by the song "Evil Woman" beginning.

But, he was writing again. There wasn't much in the world that would distract him now.

The time had passed and Michael was still pecking away vigorously. He took a second to lean back and stretch out. He pushed his arms up in the air and yawned. He had left his glasses at home, and he had been squinting the entire time. He stood from the table and walked into the kitchen. He opened the refrigerator to see what Jack had, with a rumble in his stomach starting to make itself known. The clock on the microwave read three o'clock. The house was quiet, the music from downstairs having stopped hours ago and no sign of Jack. Michael assumed he had passed out in his beanbag chair, as he hadn't come up to go to his bed.

'Maybe just a quick smoke' he thought to himself. He walked to the table and grabbed his pack of cigarettes. He searched for a lighter, but couldn't find one. He knew he had an extra in his bag back in the guest room. As he made his way back, he flipped on the light and rummaged through his bag until he found it.

Just as he shut the light off, suddenly from outside, the dog started barking emphatically. Michael stood still, knowing the only reason that dog ever barked was when someone was either coming to the front door or around back. He waited patiently for a knock to come from the living room where the front door was. Nothing. The dog still barked and barked. He waited to see if Jack would notice and react. Nothing.

He made his way down the hall to the living room. He pressed his hand against the wall, searching for the light switch. It took some fumbling, but he eventually found it and flipped the light on. Again, he waited a second. The dog still barking, he made his way to the window to have a look. He drew back the curtains and looked out to the front porch. There was no one there. He peeked over to where their cars sat in the driveway. Nothing. All the neighbors' houses sat dark and silent. The only sound was that of the beagle's constant howl.

He made his way to the stairway and yelled down to Jack. "Jack, hey man, what's with your dog?" No answer.

Michael walked to the back door, flipping on the floodlight that sat just outside. He opened the door and the dog came running toward him. The little beagle was in a panic, as it jumped up at him. Michael spoke softly to the dog to try and calm him, and also perhaps to calm himself. He made his way along the side

90

of the house to peek around the corner where the fence gate was.

He made it to the house's edge, the dog having run ahead. It was standing at the gate and barking, looking out past the gate. Michael slowly peeked his head around the corner to see if anyone was there.

He was relieved to see no one. He stepped out away from the house and over to the dog. "There's nothing there, buddy," he said, petting the dog to comfort him.

He stood up straight, and with a big sigh, lit up a cigarette. The dog began to calm down as Michael walked back under the flood light by the back door. The stars were out, and the moon was just a sliver up in the sky. He gazed upon it as he pulled another drag from his cigarette. His nerves were still a little shaky, as the dog lay down at his feet.

"Never found that ball, huh?" Michael laughed, knowing the dog wouldn't be resting if he could be playing fetch.

He finished the cigarette, flicking it off into the darkness. He turned to head back inside, when suddenly the dog jumped back up and ran for the fence gate, barking again.

"What the hell?" Michael asked, startled by the dog, thinking he was barking at nothing again.

He made his way back to the gate, reaching down to pet the dog again and reassure him.

But a voice came from the other side of the gate.

"Michael?" The voice was soft. He knew immediately, it was Amy, her voice slightly cracking as she spoke his name.

A lone streetlamp outlined her silhouette as she stood there before him.

"Amy?" was all he could say. He was in disbelief.

"Hello, Michael," she answered.

Michael held the dog back by the collar as he passed through the gate to greet her.

"Can we talk?" she asked him quietly.

"Yeah," he spoke with short breath. "Let's, uh, go to the porch."

She turned away from him and began walking around the house. Michael stood and watched her, the simple silhouette turning the corner of the house. He rubbed at his eyes, thinking perhaps this was another of his dreams.

"Michael? Are you coming?" she called back to him.

Jack had a small porch, just big enough for a small patio set sitting on it. Amy pulled out a chair and sat. Michael reached inside the front door and flipped on the porch light. Then he could fully see her, those blue eyes locked on him. Her hair was pulled back.

"Sit, please," she motioned him to the chair next to her. He complied.

"I heard you were here, and ..."

"Who told you I was here? Did my mother call you?"

She shook her head. "It's not important, Michael. I just wanted to see you again, to talk to you. Any time I run into your sisters or your mom, I ask about you."

"You do?" he asked, almost shocked by her statement.

"Yes, I do." She leaned in as she spoke again. "I'm worried about you, Michael."

He sat back in his chair, assuming that her visit was pity induced.

"I'm fine, really. Amy, I'm fine."

"No, Michael, you aren't. Look at yourself."

His heart sank. She always called him on everything. She never held back.

"When I left you, I thought there was no way you could get any worse than you were; you were so lost in your writing, you wouldn't even eat sometimes. Michael, I always admired your drive. But, look at what it's doing to you?"

Michael sat there. He didn't answer her, he just stared at his feet.

She waited for him to say something. A minute or so passed before he realized she was not saying a word until he spoke first.

"Well, it's all I know, Amy. It's all I have."

"It doesn't have to be that way, Michael. It doesn't. You simply ignore your family and friends. You can be focused and working hard, but still make time for the other things that make life what it is."

He looked at her, remembering all the nights they would have these discussions leading up to their breakup.

She took a moment before speaking again.

"That's not why I'm here, though, Michael."

He didn't answer her. He just stared back to his feet, like a small child being scolded by his mother.

She reached across to him and put her hand on top of his.

"Michael, I still love you. I miss you."

He looked up at her quickly, struggling to process what she had just said.

"Michael," she spoke as she stared deep into his eyes. "Do you ever think of me?"

He nodded, tears welling up in his eyes. She began leaning in towards him.

"I want to be with you, Michael."

She leaned in until her face was right up next to his. His eyes were locked on her. She closed her eyes and pushed her lips against his. She placed a hand on his cheek.

Michael lost himself in the kiss. He reached up as well, grabbing both sides of her face and held her in embrace.

She pulled away for just a second to ask him a question.

"Michael," she paused, "do you still love me?"

Just as Michael was about to answer, the dog began a panicked bark again. His focus broke from Amy, looking to the side of the house. He could hear the dog jumping against the fence franticly.

"What is he barking at?" he asked aloud.

Amy shook her head. More rattles of the fence came from the side of the house.

"I'll be right back," Michael told Amy as he pulled away from her. "Stay right here."

She smiled at him as he got up to run around the corner and see what had the dog in such a state. Once around the corner, the dog froze, stopping the barking and sitting stone still. Michael walked up to the fence and looked down at the dog. He sat there whisper quiet, his tail wagging and the tennis ball wedged in his mouth.

'Really?' Michael thought. 'Barking like a mad person to play fetch?'

Michael shook his head and turned his back to the dog. As he walked back around the house, he noticed that he could no longer see the ring of light on the driveway that the porch light threw out. He became frantic as he ran around the corner to see.

The porch light was off and the chairs both sat empty and neatly pushed underneath the table as if they had never been disturbed.

His breath became short, and put his hands up to his forehead in frustration.

Amy was gone again.

The sound of the refrigerator door slamming shut snapped Michael back into reality.

Jack stood there in his bathrobe and big furry bear claw slippers, a slice of pizza in hand.

"Dude, where the hell were you just now?" Jack said, having watched Michael for a bit as he daydreamed.

Michael looked down at the typewriter sitting in front of him, and the pages to stacked to his left. He had been sitting at the table the whole time.

"What time is it?" he asked Jack, confused and trying to get his bearings.

"It's like two a.m., man." Jack chuckled as he took a bite from his pizza. "Dude, you are intense when you write."

Jack walked past the table and back down the stairway again.

"Dude, E.L.O if you need a break," he yelled back at Michael, started to whistle the melody to "Strange Magic" as he made his way down the stairs.

Michael sat back in his chair, his pulse racing and his palms sweaty. He thought of Amy. It had all been a dream. Again.

Part Twelve

The morning came with very little sleep. Michael tossed and turned all night, thinking of Amy. In his mind, he tried to justify the dream due to the fact that his mother had mentioned her the day before. But that justification never truly held up. He was thinking of her because he did miss her. When his mother told him that she had spoken with Amy, he actually hoped to hear that she was miserable without him. Instead, it was only good news that his mother passed along.

He walked out into the kitchen, desperate for a cup of coffee and a cigarette. Jack was seated at the kitchen table lacing up his work boots. With a single swoop, he was up, grabbed his tool belt off of the table and threw a baseball cap on.

"I'm off to work, Mikey. There's coffee on the counter, I know you love your coffee."

"Thanks, man," Michael said, smiling. "How was E.L.O.?"

Jack stared at Michael with a 'Seriously? Are you asking me that?' look of absurdity on his face.

"Epic, man. Epic." He threw open the back door as he called back, "Have a safe trip back to the city, man. Tell your mom I said hello."

And he was off. As Michael poured himself a cup of coffee, he smiled. It was good to have a friend like Jack.

He stepped out onto the front porch. He sat and lit up a cigarette. He sipped his coffee as he thought of the dream, and of Amy. Of all the positives that this trip back home had brought, he was once again thrust back into confusion.

Another cigarette and he headed back inside. He packed up the little he had unpacked and brought his bag out and set it on the kitchen table. He pulled the suitcase that he carried his typewriter in and gently placed the typewriter inside. He took the stack of papers from and placed them neatly in a folder and added that to the suitcase.

He still couldn't shake the thought of Amy. Since he had heard of his mother's illness, he hadn't dreamt of her. Instead, his head was filled with worry and frustration. Now, thinking that he was mending fences with family, he could not stop thinking of her.

He couldn't stand it anymore. 'She'll be at work now,' he thought to himself. He reached into his pocket and pulled out his cell phone.

He called information to get her number, and he held his breath while the operator patched him through to her.

One ring. Nothing. Two rings. Nothing. Three rings. Nothing.

As the answering machine picked up, the message said: "Hey, it's Amy. I'm not here because I'm out spoiling my new nephew!! Leave a message."

His heart sank hearing her voice other than in his dreams. The beep came and he froze.

"I.. uh..." he swallowed hard. "Hey, Amy. It's Michael. Uh, I know it's been a really long time, but, uh, I am back in town visiting my mother and she mentioned that you had called to check on her. I just wanted to call and say thank you for taking the time to do that. That was really nice. And, um, maybe we can talk sometime. My number is..."

He left his number and hung up. He took a deep breath and let out a huge sigh of relief. He felt better. Now, the choice was hers whether to call or not.

He made his way back to the bathroom. He looked himself over in the mirror. He pulled his fingers through his hair. It was greasy and quite a mess, but he didn't really care. He scratched at his beard. 'Should probably shave' he thought. 'At least my lip is healed up'. He laughed, thinking of the ridiculous situation he had put himself in that night at the bar; that girl, all those drinks, and that unfamiliar feeling of being desired.

He shook his head as he stepped back out into the kitchen. He grabbed his bag and his suitcase and made his way out the back door.

The dog was waiting again, tennis ball in mouth and tail wagging. Michael laughed as the ball fell from the dog's mouth and fell perfectly at his feet. He set down his bag and picked up the ball. He chucked it to the edge of the yard and made picked his bag back up, making his way to the gate. As he latched the gate from the outside, the dog returned and dropped the ball. As Michael walked away, the dog barked after him.

'Probably cursing me' Michael thought, laughing to himself. He loaded his stuff into the back of his car and climbed in. Firing it up, he took one last look at the front porch. He could still see Amy sitting there. He pulled out of the driveway, and off down the road.

George lived about a mile out of town. He had a nice house. It was a two-story cabin back about a quarter of a mile off of the road. His lane road winded through trees, leaving his house impossible to see from the highway.

Michael pulled his car off the highway and down the lane road. He wanted to see if George was home; he knew George occasionally worked from home. He did marketing for a company that made sports equipment. It was a pretty large firm, and he was the main marketing guy for the entire market. He would work from home on days when all he had to do was call into the main national office for conference calls. The only reason Michael knew this was because it was all George talked about over Christmas dinner the last time Michael was home.

As he pulled through the trees and up to the house, he noticed the garage door was open, and George's car was parked inside.

Michael took a deep breath as he parked his car and shut it off. He had come to confront George again, and this time, try to get a word in. Bolstered by the positive outcome of last night's dinner with Rose and Lily, Michael was determined to at least be heard.

George's cabin had a big wrap-around porch. Michael walked the steps up to the porch and stepped to the door. He wiped the sweat from his palms on his pant leg and knocked on the door.

It took him a minute, but George answered the door.

He was surprised to see Michael. "Oh, Michael, hey," he said. He was much more subdued than the day before.

"Hey, George. I was hoping maybe we could talk a bit before I headed back out of town."

George sighed. "Yeah, I wanted to talk to you, too. Come on in, Michael."

Michael wasn't sure what to make of his brother's withdrawn mood. George held the door open as Michael entered. He then led Michael into the living room.

"Take a seat, Michael," George said.

As Michael sat down on George's couch, he started: "Listen, George, I know that you are upset with me. And that anger is warranted, definitely. I understand that…"

George interrupted him. "Listen, Michael, stop."

But his little brother cut back in: "No, George, I am not just going to sit here and let you steamroll me again like yesterday. I need you to hear what I have to say!"

Michael grew more animated as he grew more agitated.

But George spoke again: "Listen, just wait. I went back and visited mom last night. She told me about how the two of you spoke. She asked me to be more considerate of you and what you are going through."

Michael's head snapped back, shocked to hear George speaking so calmly.

"Okay," was all Michael could muster.

"Listen, I am so angry with you because, when you left, I

felt like you were basically deserting us. And, to be honest, you did. But, I took it very personally because I felt like I was the one left to try and keep everyone floating. You struggled with dad passing, well, imagine being the guy everyone turns to when they are hurting. Rose, Millie, Lily, and Sam all needed someone, and that was all left on me. And not to forget mom. She was not okay for a long time."

Michael watched as his brother spoke sincerely.

"You left because you needed to get away, and that's fine. But, to me, you were running from the responsibility that being in a family entails. We all needed you to be here to support us just as much as you needed to get away. And you never thought of that. You never considered it, Michael."

Michael hung his head, realizing his brother's words were true.

"That's true, George. You're right. I felt like I had to get away. From you especially."

George looked at his brother in confusion.

"You look just like him, George. Do you know how hard it was to even look at you after he died? And, kind of still is?"

George thought a moment before he spoke again. "Listen, it was a hard time for everybody. I won't deny that. But the truth of the matter is, all this time and you have just gone away. You left us hanging."

"I can't take that back, George. I wish I could go back. But to be honest, if I could go back, I don't know that I would change anything. Writing is how I cope, it how I vent. It's the only thing that keeps me going. I am sorry that I left you here to manage everyone alone. I really am. But, I can't honestly say that I would've been any help had I stayed."

"That's a cop out, Michael, and you know it."

George's face showed disgust as he listened

"That's fine if you see it that way, George. The fact of the matter is this: I can't change who I am just to appease you or anyone else. Amy left me, and I didn't change to keep her around either. I won't sacrifice who I am to make someone else happy. I'm sorry if you see that as a cop out or turning my back on you."

George was surprised at his brother's stand. He had never heard Michael speak so definitely.

"So, what you're saying is what? Take it or leave it?"

Michael thought for a moment.

"What I am saying is that this trip back home has opened my eyes to a lot of things. Perhaps, my lifestyle is not the best choice, that perhaps I have been locked inside my head for far too long. I realize that everything is changing except me. I don't really know you guys anymore, the way you all don't really know me. I know that I need to make changes. I need to come around more. The thing is, writing is not just what I do, it's who I am. When I write, I need to solitude and I need silence. I have to be off the map for a while. It's just my process."

George took a moment to let what his brother was saying sink in.

"I would love to be more like you, George. I would love to be the guy that everyone comes to when they have problems; the one that mom can depend on for anything and everything. But, I would not be as good at it as you are. My mind is too scattered and my focus is other places. Not like you, you give everything for this family."

"Don't say that, Michael. Don't say you want to be like me. You don't want to be like me."

Michael looked at George, completely not expecting to hear him say those words.

"I am nothing to strive for; I hate my job, my wife left me. This family is all I have. You, you may act like a lunatic sometimes, but you have something that you wake up for everyday. Don't ever discredit that."

George took a deep breath.

"I never wanted you to sacrifice anything just to be around more or anything. I was so angry with you because you got to get away. You had something to get away to. Not me, my only purpose was to be the one that everyone came to."

"Come on, George. Give yourself some credit here. You are that guy that always gives to everyone else over himself. I admire that about you so much."

"Well, I guess we are never meant to agree on anything, then."

George laughed. His stone face broke for a second as he chuckled. He had their father's laugh.

Michael smiled too.

George checked his watch.

"Listen, I have some calls I need to make here."

"Oh, okay. I guess you're actually on the clock here, huh?"

"Yeah." George stood and led his brother to the door.

"You're heading out pretty soon?" George asked.

"Yeah, I'm going to see mom again before I go. I have to get back and try to make a deadline."

"Well, then, I guess..." George extended his hand to Michael, "maybe I'll see you sometime soon, Michael?"

Michael shook his brother's hand.

"Hopefully sooner than later, George."

The day was warmer than yesterday, though still not as hot as he would think a normal August day would be. He drove with the windows down and caught a quick smoke as he headed back into town to see his mother.

As he passed through town, an elderly couple walked down the sidewalk toward the post office arm in arm. The man waved as Michael drove past. He smiled and waved back.

He pulled into his mother's driveway, and turned the car off.

She was sitting out on the porch, and greeted him with a smile.

"Michael, how are you?" she asked. He walked up the steps and hugged his mother.

"I'm really good, mom. I just came from George's."

"Oh, and how was that?" she asked.

"It was good. He said you spoke with him last night?" Michael playfully questioned her.

"Well, Michael, the last thing we need is George holding another grudge like he used to back in high school. He had such a temper back then. Do you remember when he punched his best friend?"

Michael laughed. "Rose, Lily and I were just talking about that last night."

"You got to see Rose, too? That's great!"

He turned the focus on her.

"How are you feeling, mom?"

"I'm pretty good so far. I don't take my pills for a few hours yet. So, I'm good for now." She was chipper, she had always been a morning person.

"Boy, I am so glad you went and spoke with George, Michael. That's such good news."

She was smiling from ear to ear.

They sat on the porch and visited for a while. She asked to hear more about Michael's new story. He obliged, going into great detail about the plot.

The time passed and the sun rose high.

"Michael, before you go, there is something I want you to take with you."

She stood from her chair on the porch and headed inside. Michael followed close behind.

"It's up in the attic," she said as she started up the stairs. He followed her up the stairs and through one of the empty bedrooms that led to the attic.

She opened the door and walked in, pulling the string on the light bulb dangling in the center of the room. She went into a box close by and reached inside. She pulled out a bound stack of papers. Michael recognized it immediately, it was a manuscript of some sort.

"Here, Michael, this is for you."

She handed him the manuscript and he opened the cover to read the title.

"Circles in My Head, by: Arthur Walker."

He looked up at his mother in disbelief.

"Your father wanted you to have this. He never knew the right time to give it to you. I thought now would be appropriate."

She smiled as she saw the sheer and utter dismay in her son's eyes.

"I don't understand, mom."

"When I met your father, we were both still in high school. His dream was to get accepted into the writing program at some big Ivy League school and become a novelist."

Michael couldn't believe what he was hearing.

"A year before we started going together, he started working on this novel. He would work on it night and day. He would break dates with me to stay and home and type away at his typewriter. There were times I thought he loved that thing more than he loved me back then."

She laughed as she told the story.

"The day we got married, we had just found out that I was pregnant with George. He vowed that day to finish the manuscript before George came along. Three years he worked on that thing before he finished, but he did. He worked so hard, just like you do, Michael."

Michael listened on, his eyes welling with tears.

"When you started writing as a boy, your father would tell me: "Martha, I sure hope he grows out of that.""

A look of confusion came over Michael's face as his mother finished her sentence.

"He knew how much of a toll it had taken on him, writing this manuscript. He wanted you to take up sports like George, and forget about writing and all the headaches that came with it."

"So, all those stories he used to tell at the barbecues?"

"Those were all made up, every single one of them. It was a trade-off, you see. Once we had children, he had to work so hard, we both did, to make ends meet. He had to give up writing because he knew he just didn't have the time to devote like he needed. So, when he told those stories at the barbecues, for a few hours, he was a writer again. Except, once everyone left, the story was over. He didn't have to worry about finishing them or getting them all down on paper. Oh, he loved telling those stories."

She slowed her speech, taking a tender moment to inhale deeply. She too was getting choked up reminiscing.

"So, he didn't want me to be a writer, then?"

"It's not that he didn't, Michael. It was that he knew what it was like. And it's exactly as you are today. You spend all your time in your own head developing characters and devising plot twists... it used to drive him crazy! But, when you won that contest after high school, he was so proud of you. He really was. It was all he could talk about, bragging to everyone that he stood in front of for more than five seconds."

Michael listened on, wanting to hear more.

"When he started to see you have success, he wanted it more than anything for you."

Michael rubbed his hand over the cover of the manuscript. "Are you sure you want me to take this? I mean,..."

"Yes, Michael. He wanted you to have it one day. And now, well, I think it's the perfect time."

"I just, I had no idea, about any of this. I always thought he was so proud of George and Sam with their sports and things, I just never thought he noticed me much growing up."

"Well, then, you are wrong Michael. He was so proud of you. You are just like he was. Do you realize how much like him you really are?"

Michael couldn't hold back the tears. His mother put her arms around him.

She stepped away, wiping the tears from her face.

"Now, that's enough of this." She was always slicing sincere moments. "You need to get back and finish this book! I am excited to read it!"

She led him back down the stairs to the front door. Michael turned back, manuscript in hand, and hugged her again.

"I love you, mom." He whispered.

"I love you too, honey."

He pulled away and started out the door.

"And mom," he turned and said, "I'll see you soon."

She smiled at him.

Then she turned serious. "You finish that book."

Michael walked the block to the grade school where Lily taught. Lighting a cigarette as he walked, he smiled as he waved to each car passing by. This whole trip was swirling about in his head. He remembered the absolute dread he felt as he packed before he left the city. And now, he felt as though he was a completely different person, happily walking through a small town he had started to think was beneath him. Now, instead, he was certain that it was just the right place to be at that very moment.

The school library was set right near the front entrance, and that familiar smell of books was the first thing to hit Michael as he walked in. Turning into the office, he asked the secretary behind the desk for Ms. Walker's room. She pointed him in the right direction, and Michael began walking down the hallway to her room.

He would peek into each room as he passed; children seated in straight rows, heads on hands and mouths open. 'Ahh, the joys of learning' he laughed to himself, remembering how often he too would daydream while in class.

Lily's room was the second to last on the right side of the building. He stuck his face in front of the glass. It didn't take long for one of the children to notice him there.

The children laughed as Michael began making faces in the window. Lily saw him there, and excused herself from the class.

"Hey, Lil," Michael said as he she stepped.

She gave him a big hug. "Michael! How are you?"

"I am great. George and I had a real conversation. And then mom gives this manuscript of dad's from before they got married. Did you know that dad was a writer?" he asked.

"I didn't, no. Mom showed me the manuscript and told me the story right after she got diagnosed. She went through this kind of 'last rites' thing where she just basically told us all her secrets. One of them was the writing. Can you believe it?"

"I was blown away. It makes sense though, those stories he used to tell at the big block party barbecues he used to throw."

"That's great, Michael. She was really excited to tell you about it. Are you heading out?"

"Yeah, just wanted to say good-bye."

She gave him another big hug.

"Love ya, Mikey," she said in a playful voice.

"You too, Lil," he answered in an equally fun voice.

"Think you'll be back any time soon?" she asked hopefully.

"Yeah, I really do. I'll give you a call when I know."

"Sounds good!"

Another quick hug and she slipped back into her classroom.

Part Thirteen

The sun beat down on his old car as he made the drive back to the city. The windows were down and the radio up, but all that was drown out as his mind was racing over the events of the trip. He smiled to himself as the miles passed by.

He was nearly halfway back when he pulled as off the interstate to gas up. He stood there, pump in hand, waiting for the tank to fill up.

Suddenly, from inside the car he could hear his phone ringing. He stopped fast. Names raced through his head of who it could be. 'George? No. Lily? No. Frank? Maybe Frank.'

He ran around the car and reached in through the open window, grabbing his phone from the center console.

He raised it to his ear: "Hello?"

The voice that answered him wasn't Frank. It was Amy.

"Michael? It's Amy."

He panicked, not expecting it to be her.

"Umm, Amy, hey there. How are you?" he fumbled over himself.

"I got your message, is this a bad time?" she asked, hearing his awkward answer.

"No, no it's fine. I'm just gassing up on my way back to the city."

"Oh, okay. Do you want to call me back when you get on the road again?"

"Ummm..." he stuttered. 'That'll buy some time' he thought. "Yes, please. Just a few minutes and I'll call you back."

"Okay, talk to you in a bit then. Bye."

She hung up. He leaned back against his car and took a deep breath. He honestly did not expect her to call back when he left the message that morning.

He made his way back around the car and pulled the gas nozzle out of the car, returning it to the pump. He got back in his car and started it up, slowly pulling out of the gas station.

His pulse raced as he searched for the right things to say. He tried to imagine the way the conversation would go, and thus prepare a perfect answer for every question she may ask.

Once back on the road, he picked up the phone again. A deep breath, then he made the call.

"Hello?" she answered.

"Amy, it's Michael."

There was an awkward pause.

"Michael, I was so glad to hear your message today. It's been so long," she started.

'Okay, she's being nice. That's a good start' he thought.

"Yeah, I was visiting my mom and I just, she told me you had called to check on her and I just thought that was so nice. I just wanted to call and thank you."

He was babbling, a nervous string of words he blurted so fast she probably didn't understand half of.

"Yeah, my mom had called me when she heard the news. How are you holding up with all of this? And the family?"

"Well, they are saying they caught the cancer pretty early. Obviously, it's never a good thing, but everyone is really optimistic."

"That's great to hear, Michael. It's good that you went and visited her."

Textbook Amy. She was very motherly.

"Listen, Michael, in your message, you said we should talk. Is there something you want to talk to me about?"

He tried to swallow the lump in his throat. He chose his words carefully.

"Well, Amy to be honest, I have been thinking about you a lot lately. And when my mom said you two spoke, she mentioned that you were in St. Louis now and had just gotten a great new job. So, I thought I would just call and hear the good news in person."

"Oh, well that's nice, Michael. Thank you. And yeah, I got this great job at a law firm here in St. Louis. It's a good job."

He laughed, knowing her definition of a "good job" is stability, not enjoyment.

"And I get to be close to my sister, she just had a baby. It's really been great for me lately."

He could hear the happiness in her voice.

"Thanks for asking, Michael."

"Well, she said you were doing well, and I just wanted you to know how happy I am that you are happy."

Amy took a beat before she spoke.

"Thanks, Michael."

"Listen, um, not be weird or anything, but this visit home has really opened my eyes about a lot of things; a lot of things that I need to change. I've been acting like a crazy person of late, and I guess I've had to face a lot of demons."

"Do you mean your father?" she asked.

She knew him better than he thought she did.

"Yeah, exactly."

"You struggled so much when he died."

"And it's not easy ever, but I understand a lot more now. Another demon was my family, how I've been neglecting them for so long. They were really mad at me."

"I know, every time I run into someone from your family, they would tell me how they worry about you and you never come around. The last time I saw Millie, she said that I was the one thing that kept you around them."

"It's true. Once you left, I had no one giving me any

direction about right and wrong. I got completely lost in my head, and wasn't worried about anyone else."

"That's what I called for, Amy. I just wanted to apologize for the way I treated you when we were together. You tried so hard so many times to connect with me, and I just wouldn't let you in."

"You don't need to apologize Michael. You never treated me badly, you were just focused. I have never met anyone as focused as you. I thought that eventually, you would slow down and take more time out for me. I was expecting you to change. So, in that respect, it was my fault."

"Nothing was your fault, Amy. Nothing. I am just sorry that things ended the way they did and that I appreciate everything you did for me and my family when we were together."

He could hear Amy's voice cracking as she spoke: "Thanks, Michael. That's really nice."

"And, I..." now Michael's voice faltered, too, "I am so happy to hear that you are doing well."

There was a moment were the only sound was that of tears being held back on both ends of the phone.

"Thanks, Michael."

"Alright, goodbye Amy."

Without giving her a chance to say anything more, he hung up the phone.

She was happy, and that was all that mattered. He smiled as he lit up another cigarette and cranked the radio. He held down the power button on his phone, just in case she would try to call back and say anymore.

He looked to the passenger seat where his father's manuscript sat. He smiled. Perhaps his father was right all along, writing is only feasible when it's all you've got. Nothing more, nothing less.

The drive home seemed to drag. He was eager to sit and read the manuscript. He was eager to see what his father toiled over for years; the reason he hoped Michael wouldn't pursue writing. The afternoon sun beat down from above as he rushed home.

It wasn't even home five minutes before he was set at his office desk, manuscript open and busily reading. When he was working steadily, Michael wrote fast and constantly. The only thing he was more proficient at was reading. He sped through the pages of his father's manuscript. He would smile to himself when he read a good line, a quick phrase, or some poignant dialogue.

He recognized the story immediately, because he had heard it a million times. Sitting on that ice chest listening to his father at the afternoon barbecues, the neighborhood men were completely entranced when he told it. His grand father had fought in the war. Michael's father's childhood was drenched in old war stories and gatherings of military men in his living room reminiscing. Veteran's Day and Memorial Day were just as celebrated as Christmas back then. Michael remembered the way his father spoke of it.

And the manuscript told it again, only in such finite detail. Aspects and scenarios his father had never gone into were there: intimate dialogue from foxholes and soldiers dying in each other's arms. The hero was his grandfather, through and through. It was fiction, but in Michael's head, his grandfather would play the part perfectly.

Breaking only to brew a pot of coffee, Michael stood at the kitchen counter. He took a moment to replay the trip. He looked about the apartment: the living room was a bunk and concrete walls. He could see a toilet in the corner and the windows had bars over them. The last few years were a blur now, spent locked away spilling his mind onto paper only to be told it wasn't good enough. 'Good enough for who?' he thought. They were long nights returning from meetings with Frank, meetings that led to the death of a project. He would read the pages over and over to find the holes that Frank had fallen through. Yet, he would always start the next day at the typewriter, ready and willing to slit his wrist and give himself completely to another project, another idea.

As the drip slowed, Michael grabbed the pot to pour himself a cup. Back down the hallway, he sat again at the desk. And he was right back into it, right back onto the beaches of Germany.

He stopped short when began Chapter 15, page 175. He sat in close and read aloud to ensure these words were his father's and not his own.

*   *   *   *   * *   *   *   *   *

"The planes would circle overhead in the early morning light there on the beach, pulling around to get to the carriers. Circles. I was mesmerized by them, the circles not the planes. I could see myself in them, fitting perfectly. They were timelines that just kept repeating. As a child, each year was a beginning and an ending. Seasons changed only to come back around again. Even my parents would change their moods (my mother was always so depressed in the gloom of February) as the days slipped away.

This war is a circle. No one is winning. We came over here in force. A lot of men died. And then, they send another wave. A limitless loop of life sacrificed. We kill ten of them, ten more file in. In January, we were winning. In February, they were winning. In March, we traded back. And so on.

I worry she has fallen into a circle as well. Each day, the army courier comes through town delivering the telegrams telling families that their soldier is dead. Each day, she holds her breath from the moment she wakes to the moment that courier passes by her house. She waits. Everyday, she waits. And I also wait to see her.

I always worry one morning, I'll wake up and those planes won't be circling. I need those planes, because any day could be the day that the circle does not complete. Something will change. Those planes are the only pacifier a soldier can know over here.

Sure, it's another day of fighting. But, it's also another day of living.

I was a proud man, after school and before the war. I believed that I could hold my head up and stand on my own; that the pitfalls of the human race were below me. I could live without circles. I would never need anyone, and no one ever needed me. I can work as hard as I want to and there is nothing weighing me down or holding me back. I was just dumb enough back then to be perfectly convinced that I was brilliant.

This war has changed me. Everyone says that: "War changes people." And, it's true. But, for me, I have become dependent on those planes. And on ole Williams feeding me the slop. And Hunter having my back knowing I'll have his.

I worry that independence will never feel safe again."

*   *   *   *   *   *   *   *   *   *

Michael sat back in his chair, the words playing again in his head. 'I was a proud man' he said to himself as he sipped at his coffee. He shook his head and laughed.

His father described him there, in that paragraph. He became lost in daydream as he looked to the suitcase that held his father's typewriter that had dropped by the door. He could see him, hunched over it as he slaved away.

There was another hundred pages or so left in the manuscript, but Michael stopped reading. He smiled as he closed it and set it to the side. Making his way down the hallway, he grabbed the suitcase and returned to the office. He was determined to dive back into what he had started, just as his father had done.

And again the scene was set: the light from the desk lamp clouded by smoke rising from a lit cigarette waiting in an ash tray next to the typewriter Michael was hunched over. The only sound was an echo of keys slamming letter after letter. The pages began stacking up on the table and he only broke to get another cup of coffee.

PART FOURTEEN

Hours had passed, and as Michael rubbed at his eyes to try and wake himself, the phone began to rang in the kitchen. That familiar reaction of 'Who the hell is that?' came over him. But then, he felt himself drawn to answer it, hoping maybe it was one of his siblings.

He walked down the hall and picked up the receiver.

"Hello?" he answered.

"Michael? Glad I caught you. Did I wake you?"

He recognized the voice as Frank.

"No, no, Frank. You didn't wake me. I was just working."

"Well, that is great news. I wasn't sure if you'd be back in town yet."

"Yeah, got in…" he paused, having lost track of time while writing, he wanted to check the microwave before he could accurately answer the question. It read 8:35. He assumed it meant in the morning. "Yesterday, I guess."

"Well, that's even better news. You don't even know what time it is. Listen, I just wanted to check in with you and see if there was any progress happening."

"Yeah, actually. I have been working pretty steady and am getting close. I would say maybe another week tops."

"Really? That would be perfect. I don't want to rush it, Michael. I talked with the publishers and they are looking at a January release date. That would give us a month to get it into editing and proofing."

Frank's surprise came as a bit of a comfort to Michael. He had been shocked by Frank's reaction when he took the trip.

"That should be no problem, Frank."

"Well, that sounds perfect, Michael. I'll be in touch, and if anything changes just let me know. We'll setup a meeting when it's done."

"Sounds good, Frank."

As Michael hung up the phone, he smiled. He had been convinced that the trip back home could have meant a problem with the book, and more importantly, Frank. But, now, he was back to working and still in Frank's good graces.

He was nearly back to the office when there was a knock at the door.

"Mikey!" came calling from the hallway on the other side of the door.

'Vince' Michael thought.

He rushed down the hall to let him in.

As the door opened, Vince walked right in without an invitation.

"That was quick this time. Normally takes me ten minutes of yelling before you drag yourself away."

"Just got off the phone with the editor. And, make yourself at home, Vince," Michael said, closing the door.

Vince was pacing the living room fumbling around his pocket.

"Editor, huh? You got one cooking there, Mikey?"

Michael could see the dollar signs lighting up Vince's eyes.

"Does this mean..." Vince rolled his eyes as he spoke, "perhaps, an upgrade in the near future?"

"I don't think so, Vince. Just the usual will do."

Vince pulled the baggie out of his pocket and set it on the coffee table.

"I forgot you were coming, so let me go get some cash."

As Michael walked down the hall to the bedroom, Vince called after him.

"So, this one gonna be a hit, Mikey? I mean, best-seller stuff or what?"

"Can't really say," Michael answered back, rifling through his drawers looking for the old cigar box where he kept cash hidden. "My editor thinks it will be something."

"Well, that's good, Mikey. I gotta be honest with ya, it's been rough coming around here, lately."

Michael returned to the living room, and handed Vince a wad of cash.

"Yeah, well, I guess we all go through that from time to time, huh?"

Vince laughed, counting the money and shaking his head.

"What's funny? Is that not right?" Michael asked, thinking he counted the money wrong in his rush.

"No, no," Vince said, still laughing.

"Then what are you chuckling about?" Michael questioned again.

Vince started walking for the door, shoving Michael's cash into his wallet. He shoved the wallet into his pocket, and turned back to Michael as he opened door.

Michael still looked at him, still puzzled.

"Guess I never took you for a 'circle of life' kind of guy, that's all, Mikey."

Vince closed the door behind him, and Michael could hear him laughing all the way down the hallway.

'Me neither' he thought to himself and laughed.

The trails in the carpet that ran down the hallway only grew more worn over the next week. Michael slept minimally as he finished the book. It was writing, coffee, writing, cigarettes, writing. He would still take his afternoon breaks when Sarah would come home with her kids. But, he would spend the time re-reading his father's manuscript instead of just lost in his mind.

The calendar had slipped into September when he finally sat up from the typewriter and set the last sheet on top of the pile. He smiled as he lit another cigarette. He rose from his desk and walked to the window. Night had fallen, and the rings of the streetlamps were the only lights on the street. All the windows in the neighboring apartments were out. 'Must be late' he thought to himself. Puffing again at the cigarette, he exhaled one great big sigh.

He was finished. Celebration was never something he had much time for. The day he finished his first novel, the publishing deal was already done. He was eager to start working on another book, and literally delivered the finished manuscript to Frank only to return home and sit back down at the typewriter. The last time he celebrated, he ended up flat on his back in the alley between two bars with a brute of a young man standing over him.

He smiled as the memory of that night came to him. He could see the girl nuzzled up next to him in the booth. Then, the large black shadow of the man fell onto them. He laughed.

The morning would bring the phone call to Frank, followed by the meeting to deliver the manuscript. He knew it was late, but we was never really "tired", at least not to the effect of sleeping. His eyes continued to scan the street. As they made their way down to the corner, he saw the neon light from the diner glowing.

He thought of Sarah, standing there at the counter, white uniform and her hair disheveled. He crossed the room and turned out the desk lamp perched above the typewriter. He walked down the hall and put on his shoes. He lit a cigarette as he made his way down the hall to the elevator.

A breeze filled the street as he stepped out into it. The air was still warm, and he dodged in and out of the streetlights as he walked down the street. Taxicabs slowed as they passed him, but he just waved them by. He laughed as he thought to himself 'I guess only drunks are out this late'.

The bell rang out as he stepped into the diner. He scanned the place, spotting the booth he sat the first night tucked back in the corner and empty. It was pretty quiet there, only a tables full and a few seats at the counter taken. As he walked across the diner, he checked each waitress's face to try to find Sarah.

As he sat in the booth and got settled, he was greeted.

"Well, well, well. Look what we have here."

He smiled as he recognized her voice. It was Sarah.

She walked up to the table, taking a moment to pull the hair that had fallen back into her ponytail. She still wore that white uniform, the long day showing on it by way of food stains in various colors and sizes.

She smiled as she spoke again. "Long time, no see, stranger."

"Well, yeah, sorry," Michael began, smiling back at her. "But, with good reason."

"Did you finish the book?" she asked eagerly.

"About ten minutes ago," Michael answered proudly.

"Well, we should celebrate!" she exclaimed.

She quickly turned around and darted back into the kitchen. A few minutes passed and then she returned with a large dish in her hand. She returned to his table and set the dish down in front of him.

"A congratulatory hot fudge sundae, compliments of yours truly."

He sat back and smiled. He shook his head and he joked: "Don't you guys have a bigger one?"

She laughed. The sundae was clearly portioned for an entire football team to enjoy.

"So, tell me more. When will it be out? Do you know?"

"Well, they talked about January, granted the re-writes and proofing go quickly."

"That's so exciting," she grabbed his wrist as she spoke.

Michael felt like a schoolboy getting praise from his teacher. He was a bit overwhelmed by it all.

"I wanted to say thank you, also," Michael began. "Perhaps, I should get you a sundae as well."

"Thank me, for what, Michael?" She looked puzzled.

"You were kind to me."

He could tell she wanted to interject, but instead she just stood and listened.

"I gave you a million reasons to hate me, to loathe me. But, I come in here and you were so kind to me."

She looked on, as if no one had spoken to her so sincerely before.

"I was in a bad spot, well, to be honest, I had been in a bad spot for a long time. But, you talked with me. You helped me realize that there are things more important, things worth taking time for."

She seemed stunned. He waited for a reaction, but she stood there frozen, listening.

"My mom is sick. I found out and I was actually debating, debating about whether I should go home to see her or stay and finish this book. Then, we spoke and you said 'Family is everything.' And it clicked, as if I didn't know that. As if, it never occurred to me that other things can be important. So," now he reached up and grabbed her hand, "thank you."

Sarah was silent. She was frozen. For a moment, Michael waited for her reaction. He waited.

"You're welcome, Michael."

Michael took a big spoonful and shoved it into his mouth. Sarah laughed, as the hot fudge capped the corners of his mouth a whipped cream dot sat on his nose.

"Well, I'll let you to it, then," she started, turning away. "Let me know if you need anything else."

She smiled and walked away. Michael continued on his sundae with the grin of a child in a candy store.

PART FIFTEEN

The taxicab pulled up to the corner, splashing water from a puddle up onto his shoes. Sometime over night, it had started to rain. Michael stood there in his gray suit waiting. He opened the door and climbed in, shaking off the newspaper he was using to for shelter from the rain. "Chestnut and 5th," was all he said to the cab driver. He picked his tie up from where it laid against his shirt. He looked it over; there were a few stains peppered on it from the bar fight. He laughed. He was heading back to that bar.

The clock over the bar read just past noon as he walked into the bar. He scanned the room for Frank, only to find him in the usual state: corner booth with two gin and tonics sitting in front of him. Frank waved him over.

"Michael, good to see you." He stood and greeted Michael with a firm handshake.

"Likewise, Frank. And so lovely that it could be on such good terms," Michael joked.

"Well, I must admit that drop off meetings are always a bit more lighthearted."

Michael lifted the suitcase he was carrying up onto the seat next to him. He popped it open and pulled out the folder that held his manuscript. He handed it across the table.

"There it is. I did some scanning, I don't think the proofer will have too much of a task with it."

Frank flipped through the pages and smiled.

"Looks great to me." He looked over at Michael, "Then

again, finished manuscripts can't possibly look like anything but great."

Frank grabbed the glass set in front of him and raised it, proposing a toast. Michael followed in turn.

"To the best-seller list and your continued success."

They clinked glasses and drank.

"I have to be honest with you, Frank, this couldn't have come at a better time."

Frank laughed, as if he knew exactly what Michael meant.

"I might have been going crazy trying to find a good story."

"I admit that I worried about you, Michael. But, I knew with the quality of your first novel that it wasn't the only story you had to tell."

The moment of joy was cut short when Frank looked to his watch.

"Oh, well, I hate to cut this short, but if I get this to the publisher by one o'clock, they'll have it in a proofer's hands before the end of the day."

As he rose from the table, he downed the drink in front of him. He extended a hand to Michael as he picked up the manuscript with the other.

"A pleasure, as always, Mr. Walker."

Michael laughed as Frank hustled out of the bar. It was always very funny to Michael to watch businessmen in a hurry; their expensive designer suits and shiny shoes. It was just very unnatural looking for them to be rushing about.

But, to that effect, Frank was always rushing around. Michael sipped away at his drink. He looked about again; the place was nearly empty other than a few seats at the bar. They were two burly men with beards much thicker than his. They wore flannel shirts and work boots. Michael began formulating back-stories for them, as he often did when he actually went out into public. He imagined: they were construction workers working on the new parking lot the city was putting it at the downtown library, but the rain cut the day short so they were having a few before heading home to their nagging wives. They joked a lot about their wives, as if they were the bane of their existence, and a few cold beers was the only possible remedy.

It wasn't long until Michael grew bored with them. Once again, he returned to scanning the room. Just he came across the front door, it swung open and three young women came walking in. They looked to be college girls, loud and fresh-faced. They were laughing and pouring over each other as they made their way to the bar. Two of them were blonde girls and the third had dark hair. Once they had their drinks, they moved to a table in the center of the bar. Michael began to focus in more closely on them, starting to daydream their stories in his mind.

As they settled in, the two blonde girls were facing him, while the dark haired girl had her back to him. One of the girls noticed him watching them, and motioned for the others to look. When the dark haired girl turned about, Michael recognized her.

He quickly looked away, seeing that it was the girl from the night of the last meeting: the one with the boyfriend with a jealous streak.

Unfortunately, she remembered him as well. She perked up when she saw him, and immediately jumped up from her chair. She crossed the bar and walked up to his table.

"Hello, again. Do you remember me?" she asked.

Michael looked up at her, realizing he had no other choice.

"Oh, hey there. Yes, I do remember you."

"Don't worry, there won't be trouble this time. I dumped that jerk after that night. I felt so bad, he's such an infant acting like that. I wanted to apologize, but it got so hectic and then you took off so fast that I..."

Michael interrupted her. "Listen, there's no need for any of this. The past is just that." He nodded to her further his point.

"That's so nice of you to say. I mean, I thought we were

having a nice time before all that happened."

She smiled at him. Michael began to feel a bit uneasy.

"To be honest, I have thought about you a lot. I mean, I absolutely loved your book, and I'd love to sit and talk more about it with you."

She was playing with her hair, twirling it between her fingers.

Michael didn't have time to answer her, as she sat down across from him.

She reached for his empty glass. "What are you drinking? We should get you another one." She leaned across the table toward him. Nothing she was doing would be defined as subtle.

Michael stopped her short.

"Actually, I was just heading out."

Her face turned stern.

"Oh," she said. "You can't stay for a little while?"

Michael spoke: "No, no. I really have to be going."

"Well, maybe I could give you my number and we can get together sometime. I would love to pick your brain. You know, I actually pushed my professor to put your novel on the reading list."

"Well, that was very nice of you." Michael was finding it harder and harder to deflect his temptation to stay.

She started writing her number down on the napkin she pulled from under his glass. She slid it across the table to him.

He picked it up and stood from the table.

She stood as well, moving in close to him as she did so.

"Well, it was great to see you again," she said, slightly leaning even more.

"Yes, it was good to see you as well."

Michael reached into the seat to grab his suitcase and turned away from her.

As he stepped out onto the street, he crumpled the napkin in his hand and threw it into a trashcan on the curb.

He started on down the street, watching for taxis to hail to get back home. He lifted his suitcase over his head to stay out of the rain.

He knew the feeling. He sat on the couch and tried to focus long enough to watch a full episode of Seinfeld. It was the same with every show that came on after that, too. He had been going back and forth with the editor at the publishing house, making changes and getting the manuscript ready for press.

With his first book, Michael was sure that he would go crazy. The entire process was all waiting and almost no work. The publisher asked for a very minimal amount of changes, so there would be weeks gone by without a single thing done on Michael's end.

He had been spending a lot of time calling his family, staying in touch and keeping them posted on the process. He stood from the couch and headed into the kitchen where he picked up the phone.

He dialed and it rang: once, twice, three times.

"Hello."

"Mom, hey, it's Michael. How are you?" he asked.

She sounded happy to hear from him. "Oh, Michael, hello there! I am good. How about you? Have you head anymore from the publisher?"

"Nope, not yet. Frank said they were close to sending me the next round of changes. How was your doctor's visit today?"

"Well, you know, they do some poking and prodding. I'm sure they mean well, but it's a bit obnoxious." She laughed.

She had been in good spirits the last few times they had spoken.

"And you haven't been feeling too sick lately?"

"Well, it comes and goes, Michael. Some days are a lot worse than others. But, that's all part of it."

"Yeah, well, I'm glad to hear you are feeling okay."

"Have you spoken to your brothers and sisters lately?" she asked.

"Well, Millie and Sam are always moving around. I did get a hold of Sam once and we chatted for a while. Mostly, it's just George, Lily and Rose. But, yeah, I call them all every once in a while."

"I'm glad to hear it, Michael. I really am. Well, maybe you should give George a call. I think he had a job interview today."

"Oh, yeah, he told me about that. What was it, something at a book store, or something?"

"Yeah, it's a management position. He said he wanted to do something completely different. I was kind of surprised myself."

"Well, yeah, I'll give him a call later on tonight then."

"Well, alright, son. I'm proud of you, and let me know when you hear from the publisher."

"Okay, mom. Will do. Love you."

"Love you too, sweetie."

He wandered back to the couch after hanging up the phone. He looked back to check the microwave clock: 3:15 pm. He knew that no news by five o'clock meant it was another day of waiting.

Just as he got back to the couch, the telephone rang.

He sprung up to answer it.

"January 22nd."

It was Frank.

"What's that?" Michael asked, not having caught what Frank had said.

He said it again, this time drawing the words out very slowly.

"They loved it. They had a few ideas, but I fought them off. They are sending it to make the final manuscript. Once approved, it's off for publishing."

"That's great!" Michael let out a big sigh. Relief washed over him.

"There you go. Now you can sleep tonight."

"Oh, man, that is such great news! Frank, thank you so much!"

"Alright, I'll ship the final over to you as soon as I get it. Congratulations, Michael, you are officially a two time published author."

With that, he hung up the phone.

Michael took a moment to let it sink in before he picked the phone right back up.

One ring. Two rings.

"Hello?"

"Lily! Guess what!"

"Michael! What?"

"January 22nd is the release date. I just got off the phone with my editor."

"That's such good news, Michael. Have you called anyone else yet?"

"Nope, you are the first. I'm going to call mom now. Then the rest later on tonight."

"Well, that's such great news, Michael."

He hung up the phone and frantically dialed his mother's number again.

"Hello?"

"Mom, my editor just called. January 22 is the release date."

"Michael, that's wonderful news. They didn't want any more changes then?"

"Nope. It's ready for pressing!"

"Let me write that down. January 22," she spoke as she wrote it down. "I had an idea, Michael."

"Yeah, what is it?"

"Remember when you won that contest and got to go to New York City? Do you remember the party your father had for you?"

"Yeah, I do. That was really nice."

"I thought maybe we'd have another party for you for this book. What do you think?"

Michael got a bit choked up. He stood there for a minute, the memories of his father standing right at his side that whole day back then flashing in front of his eyes.

"Michael?" she asked after he didn't answer her.

"That would be really nice, mom. Thank you."

"Okay, I'll get it going. That's such great news, Michael."

He hung up the phone and leaned against the counter; the flashes of his father still in his eyes. He smiled.

PART SIXTEEN

Circles. It all came back to circles. He sat in his office with his father's manuscript in front of him, reading it again. He kept returning to the excerpt that first made his breath short: Chapter 15, page 175. When he squinted his eyes, the words seemed to almost spell out his name. His father had sat in his seat once, toiling and squinting, on the brink of a nervous breakdown.

Now that the bridges between him and his family were beginning to be mended, Michael wondered if that which he so boldly opposed, those circles that life develops into, will be coming down the line; coming for him like the prison guards chasing a fugitive. They got to his father. He wondered if his father had fought as hard as he did to keep them at bay.

He thought of the barbecues, and the ice chests he perched himself on, and the hours he would spend listening to his father tell his stories. All along, that was how he wrote his books. But, he was a happy man; he had his family, his work, his duties and responsibilities. As long as he had those barbecues, he had never fully given up on writing.

Satisfaction was playing on the jukebox that night as the pretty girl poured over his fame. But, Michael never really knew satisfaction; he never really knew happiness. He was engulfed in his writing so much, that he never took the time to enjoy those things "happy" people did. Even when he was with Amy, he never really connected enough to love her. He said it often, as did she. But, that was mostly because that's what people say. He knew he didn't really feel it, and often wondered how she could.

When they published his first book, there was no time taken to relish in the accomplishment. Instead, he felt this immense pressure to write more, as if he had to prove the first book wasn't a fluke. He had been chasing that ghost for years now, and finally, he had caught it. But, the moment was fleeting.

Even as he sat and read, he felt the tingling in his fingers that always came when he had been dormant for more than a few days. With the proofing process, he had barely written anything in weeks. But, the changes were made and the book was done.

He thought of his mother, standing over his father's casket the day they buried him. She wept so hard. 'What if he had stuck to his guns?' he wondered. 'What if he kept writing instead of settling down and getting married?' It was hard for him to imagine his mother without his father. They worked well together: her gentle voice and calm demeanor against his stern stance and firm tone. 'What if he didn't change?'

The questions he posed to himself were not inquiries into his father's life, but his own. He had made big strides in reconnecting an actual life with his existence. His family was slowly warming to him again, and he was spending less time stuck in his own head. Perhaps, in fact, circles are unavoidable. Perhaps the notion that working to stay out of falling into patterns was, in itself, the biggest circle of all.

He set his father's manuscript off to the side and stared at the typewriter in front of him. He set his fingers to the keys.

"Every man can change, no matter how long it takes. Patience and persistence."

He smiled as he read the words back. He thought of his mother, the way she spoke bluntly, yet softly. And of George, the spitting image of his father.

Though he was starting to see clearly again, he lit a cigarette. The smoke rose up and blurred the words on the page. He stood from the desk and pulled a stack of paper from a ream sitting in the corner. As he sat back at the desk, he pulled a fresh ribbon from one of the drawers to his right. Quickly changing it out, he walked down the hallway to throw the old one in the trash. He fumbled around in the cabinet for the coffee and filters. He filled the pot and started the pot brewing. Puffing heavily on the cigarette, he looked into the living room where the TV set played; another infomercial, this one for an electric fireplace. He smiled as he watched as the pot brewed.

With a fresh cup of coffee in hand and a cloud of smoke trailing him, Michael walked back down the rough groove of carpet that led back to his office. He sat at the desk and quickly started typing away again.

He was never satisfied. And so began another unavoidable circle, like those planes flying overhead on that beach in Germany so long ago. And just as his father had, he had yet another story to tell.

Made in the USA
Columbia, SC
23 June 2023

18763731R00075